Another Lust

TKO

Volume 1

Authored by Jae Jameis

Writer: Jermaine Johnson

Graphic Art: Janell Hollis

Cover Design: Jae Jameis

First Thoughts

Writing a book about your life, you never realize how much life you've really lived, so when I made the decision to write this book, I figured ok simple enough just write what happened. No, not so fast, I began to understand I had to present proper transitions and skip certain details to avoid the reader getting caught up in the minutia of a trip to Las Vegas or in person who really didn't contribute to the entertainment of you, the reader. Which coincided with the fact I was writing about a part of my life not the whole of my story from that time period. The last point, which at first was disappointing because I wanted you the reader to not feel like this was just a tale of fantasy or some "flight of fancy". I had to change names and dates to create characters, which protected the people near my story and myself as well. To my chagrin once I contacted a publisher, he let me know that the book would have to be categorized as fiction, because I changed names and dates. For a second I thought well there goes one of the unique aspects of my book, but then I thought about it, I said to myself this is my book, I can talk to you the way I want and ultimately it would be up to you to decide true or not, whether you love the story. So, I present to you a story based on real events, a diary of thoughts, included; the lessons I learned, the funniest incidents I've encountered during this time, my proudest moments, and the moments I'm not so proud of. My hope is that you read this story with an open mind. I didn't embark on this journey to tell a story that has been told before, I felt like this story was funny, new, fresh, something that even a person who doesn't like to read would find themselves enjoying or something that would make an avid reader fall in love with, who knows maybe help someone along the way, but most importantly it's my story, so of course I think it's a story worth telling.

Prologue

Certainties in life work one of two ways it can either be a source of peace, making someone feel safe and secure or it can make a person feel trapped, like they've reached their full potential, life is set, now there's nowhere else to go but down, and when you're not ready that can be a frightening thought. I believe subconsciously that could explain a lot of the reasoning behind the decision to get married or divorced, of course that's not all there is to marriage and divorce but it's something that I think permeates through every decision in life. When presented with a possible certainty, how do we perceive it? We have all heard the line from Benjamin Franklin in some way shape or form, when he famously wrote in a letter referencing the nations declaration of independence, "in this world nothing can be said to be certain but death and taxes". Undoubtedly Ben may have been paraphrasing from others before his time, but the idea remained the same, even today people say it, the two things in this world that you can count on are "Death and taxes". It's true, it's something we all experience, whether you figure out a way to claim every last kid you know, Uncle Sam will collect at some point, no matter how big your refund is or how much you make, whatever you purchase, it's going to get taxed. I'll tell the truth I pay my credit cards down and all the taxes and interest on the stuff I don't remember purchasing, then as a reward for being responsible I treat myself to buying something that's well ...taxed, so yeah the tax man will always have his day. As for death well that's self-explanatory, it's the cruelest part of life, we all have or will lose a loved one at some point whether it's a friend, family, or even a pet. Hell, one day our number will be called, and it will hurt our loved ones just like it hurt us when we experienced loss. With that being said, Benjamin Franklin and all greater or lesser minds for that matter who believe life certainties are only reserved for death and taxes are wrong, they're one certainty short and that certainty is love, that's what they missed. But before you roll your eyes and put the book down, listen. I'm not the big romantic type, I believe chivalry is a situational proposition and should be used wisely, to put it frankly, I'm a realist, but that's exactly what brought me to this conclusion, so hear me out if you will. Now I know what some of you are thinking " I don't love nobody but my kids " or "I just love my mom and my money" or "my bed and my money" blah, blah, blah. The point is you love something, most likely someone at some point and if you were lucky enough someone loved you back. I vaguely remember this time I was on a retreat and the [1]speak er presented a book about *"The language of love"* or "Love languages" where I can only assume the author meant to explain the different ways to navigate loving a new flame or significant other, but I was more focused at the time on the food and extracurriculars, I probably should've paid more attention, that seminar might have saved me from a few hiccups in life, leaves me wondering if that book was on to something.

Love comes in many forms and is displayed in just as many ways, if not more. There's the unconditional familial love, the type you have for a mother, brother, child or a close friend. Subjective love, as I like to call it, you love what something does for you, whether it's money, a person who's always there for you or the love of a hobby that makes you feel complete. Then there's the most popular type of love, the romantic love that we all hear about. The love between two people that may involve all the facets of the types of love said before, but as we all know infinitely more complex than the straightforward nature of loving your sister or loving your favorite vacation spot. From any Disney princess story to your daily soap operas it usually revolves around romantic love, it's a damn Disney movie I think to myself sometimes. I guess the world figures we have to get em' young. A story was made about death, *Meet Joe Black* back in 1998, where death fell in love. Only love can make this shit up. Death fell in love! Meet Joe Black, great movie, with an ironic scene in it about death and taxes, but death falling in love? Only love can make nonsense make sense. I could only imagine where the line *love will make you do crazy things* came from. Somewhere someone experienced this very thought, maybe observing a close friends behavior after they met that "special someone" or they themselves were experiencing that complex part of love and thought aloud, "love will make you do crazy things" right before they in fact, did something "crazy" , which always makes for a great story, yes tragic at times like Romeo and Juliet but a story worth telling nonetheless.

Love will make you do crazy things, but why? Some will give you a religious without God in your relationship you're not grounded, then this then that reasoning, or a biological hormonal reason and how it affects your emotions overriding your usually "good judgment". Ok we can go with that, no disagreement here with either of those points, but let me add a little something to those schools of thought

7

with this thought. One of the hardest parts of love is recognizing it, how do you know if you're in love, lust, infatuated, or just in strong like? How do you conduct yourself accordingly, and can true love grow from pure lust or attraction? The answer is yes. Love can most likely grow between anyone, anywhere or in any of these situations but how do you recognize when it hasn't grown or when it doesn't even stand a chance to? I think that's the part that drives people crazy, well makes them do crazy things anyway as the saying goes. For the remainder of this revealing personal testimony, excuse me, a story "based on true events", it will be fair to usually assume the love I am speaking of is of the romantic type and how good I am at recognizing it............Hopefully you picked up on my sarcasm just then because the last part about me being good at recognizing love is about as much bullshit as bullshit can get, I'm just as bad at it as all of you are. Figuring out what's in front of you, love, lust or whatever you're experiencing is vital, it protects you from wasting valuable time, effort, money, sweat and tears, hell it's as important as it would be for a prize fighter in the ring being able to recognize a hook from a jab, a hook from an uppercut, a jab from a hard straight, or the proper distance to keep with an opponent, failure to do so in the ring as in love, will more than likely result with you being put square on your ass, dazed and confused wondering how you got there. Thinking how did I get caught with that? I should have seen that coming while simultaneously blaming the person that hurt you because you most certainly couldn't be that big of a sucker, especially not when you prepared yourself for the bullshit and you did everything right. Think of it like when a boxer gets hit clean and he gets hurt or knocked down and he looks at the ref and as he tries to recover, he rubs or draws attention to the back of his head signaling, "Hey I just got hit with an illegal blow", and the world watching is just like sorry man it was a clean shot. You just got…. got.

Funny thing, when you closely examine life and love, it's so like the sport that bind my best friends and I together. I recall so many times watching a boxing match, you see a fighter in trouble or it's just not his night, he survives the round, he returns to his corner, plops down on the stool and you see the look on his face. He just wants to go the distance. He's more concerned with not getting hurt or knocked out. He wants to win but, "he doesn't want it". He's not hungry. With a glazed look over his eyes he nods his head to his corner's instructions, seemingly ready to turn the tide and give us something to cheer for. Giving us that Rocky Balboa moment, but then he

9

goes out and does the same damn thing that's been losing him the fight the last seven to eight rounds, you finally realize he's content with just making it to the next bell. Regardless of the great instruction from his corner telling him exactly what he needs to do to win. Ultimately, it's up to the fighter to execute, and even then, it doesn't matter what we see or what his corner sees, nobody has a more intimate knowledge of the fight happening in real time than the two fighters involved. A fighter knows if he is quick enough to get to a spot once the action starts, the other fighter knows it too. Fighters know whether they can take the punishment to force the action, or if deep down they are unwilling to, so with all the great instruction from someone's corner it's just lip service in some cases, flat out waste of breath, but you have to try he's your fighter. How many of us have felt the frustrations of a fighter's corner? I know I have. How many of us have been that fighter, content in their situation silently resigned to the result, ignoring all advice and wisdom from true close friends and loved ones in your corner that have your best interest? I have. Someone can tell you, "Hey girl, if a man wants you, he will make it happen" but what does making it happen look like coming from him specifically? Who really knows but him? Are you willing to accept that he may not want you like you want him to, and move on, or are you content stringing yourself along knowing that he may never be able to emotionally provide you with what you need but you just want him, so you stick around settling? Men when your boy tells you, "Bruh, I wouldn't trust her", can you be objective and not fall for the "rope a dope", and the situations can be reversed it's not gender specific. I know we think we can dodge that hook we're being set up with or the energy we are putting forth is really doing the job because as a man or a woman we have to make sense of the tireless, seemingly well-thought out effort we're putting in to someone or something, so we press forward......... ask George Foreman how that worked out in Zaire. The music group Main Ingredient said it best, "Everybody Plays the Fool".

Love and fools doing foolish things is a story we all have to tell, but this is mine. I give you me, my story, the loves I've lost, the lust I fell for, the mistakes I've made, the heartbreak I've caused, the fun I have had along the way and my boys who have been with me in my corner through all the low blows, near misses, and knock downs. Now, I can't promise you will love me or what characters you will root for, if any. This book isn't written for that, real life doesn't always give us a perfect character. So I'm going to try my best not to tell you how to think or what to do, but it is my hope while reading this you will laugh a lot, maybe cry a bit and see yourself at some point in someone in this book, maybe for understanding of the present, to let go of the past, to forgive someone or possibly forgive yourself, or maybe it's just a good story, hopefully this reading accomplishes all of the above.

Chapter I

How fun is this?!

After a long day of work, I have to say, it's great as a husband to be able to go home to your family and relax. Before you even get the key in good, you hear your kids running to greet you before you walk in. Like they were waiting all evening just to hear you turn the key, you open the door and they see you. Watching their face light up is the best. Then, talking to your wife about your day, then hearing about hers, it's one of the simple pleasures in life that I try not to take for granted.

Door opens, "Hey baby"

Wife: *Hey, do you know a Nickita Wilson?*

Me: Um yea, yea that's one of my friends, I work with her. Why what's up?

Wife: *What's up!? What the fuck is up with y'all talking and texting so much especially when you don't text me but once or twice a day?*

Me: Hold up, slow down, stop tripping we in the same profession so we talk about work a lot.

Wife: *Shut up with yo' lying ass, you think I'm stupid? Her address is 102 Wooten ......*

Me: Ok and you telling me this because?

Wife*: Because bitch yo' phone GPS has you at that location at least two times.*

Me: Wait what hold up when?

Wife: *Why does it matter when?*

Because I just had to drop something off to her, just some work-related stuff.

Wife: *Work related? ....*

Me: Yes!

Wife: *Well why the fuck didn't you give her that shit at work, since y'all motherfuckers work together? You had to drop something off, right? Yes?*

Me: Yea.

Wife: *What the fuck were you dropping off to her at 1 am and 11:50 at night when me and the kids was at my daddy's house, some dick!? Is that what the fuck you was dropping off?*

Me: No! the hell you talking bout?!

Wife: *What the fuck am I talking bout, oh you don't know? You lying cheating ass motherfucker! Why the hell you got these pictures in yo' phone, is this her? That's what the fuck I'm talking bout! You aint shit you dirty motherfucker.*

Me: No...... I mean yeah but it's not like that, at work we had to submit pictures for the online directory, I had an iPhone, you know iPhone got the best camera, so I was just being nice, and I let her use it.

Wife: *Oh, you had the good camera?*

Me: Yea!

Wife: *Shut the fuck up why you lie so got damn much?*

Me: Ain't nobody lying!

Wife: *So, you mean to tell me, you the only motherfucker at work with an iPhone and you jackass I aint dumb this shit look like a selfie, so you telling me, this ugly big face ass heffer used these pictures for the directory? Show me then, right fucking now!*

 Me: Why are you tripping, what's the problem?

Wife: *The problem?! The problem is you a cheating lying sorry ass son of a bitch, show me the directory motherfucker! Five years and you pull this shit, I deserve this? I have been nothing but good to you, what about your family did you think about that shit when you were fucking her!?*

Me: Baby I wasn't messing with nobody I swear!

Wife: *You risked it all for some bitch who don't respect me, you, or your family.*

Me: What!?

Wife: *What! My ass, are you really going to hold on to that lie?*

Me: Baby I...

Wife: *You really going to hold on to that fucking lie?!*

Me: I....

Wife: *You really going to hold on to that motherfucking lie!?!*

Me: Wait hold on why you cussing like this? Where the kids at?

Wife: *Don't worry about that shit, you need to worry about you, with yo' lying ass.*

Me: No, where my kids!?

Wife: *Oh, now you worried about your kids!*

Me: Yo, stop playing and answer the damn question.

Wife: *Oh, so now yo lying ass wants some questions answered. How convenient. They at my daddy's!*

Me: Why the hell my kids aint at home?

Wife: *Because we out, you dirty bastard, with yo lying cheating ass.*

17

Me: Y'all out? What's that supposed to mean you can't take my fucking kids nowhere!

Wife: *Oh, I can't huh? Well too late you should have thought about that shit before you started fucking that bitch!*

Me: I wasn't fucking nobody, shit!

Wife: *You gone keep lying ain't you, man up and tell the truth, you was man enough to do it, man up and tell the truth.*

Me: Ok, listen...

Excuse me, if I may interject in the middle of this. Don't worry. We'll get back to this later, but I have to say my peace uninterrupted. She is uncontrollable right now. Things were so much easier when I was in college. There's nothing like having the freedom of walking into your dorm, apartment or whatever, and not having to deal with the bombardment of questions and the responsibility of someone else's feelings affecting your day, let alone your life. It's one of the simple pleasures in life I tried never to take for granted. I mean don't get me wrong at this point I was a married young professional with two kids. I found out there's another bundle of joy on the way, my wife has a great job as a nurse practitioner. I'm a young assistant administrator in my company's human resource office. Life couldn't be more setup for success, really at this point, I'm a success by most standards. There's just one thing...I'm on the verge of divorce, well at this point in my life where you guys are picking up, I'm pretty sure I'm getting divorced. Did I mention how much easier things were in college and way more fun, I don't know why I ever left.

Marriage, kids, divorce all were such abstract and distant ideas back then. College was too much fun and I was too young, a Wednesday night for me in college, meant potential fun and if there wasn't any fun to be had we made it, like one weeknight we were bored so we decided to ride around campus in *Scream Masks* with a bag full of water balloons, let me take a moment to say if you're reading this and you're the young lady we got that night with a cascade of water balloons, I apologize. I do still laugh about it, we were young and so dumb, so ma'am I hope you still aren't harboring any hard feelings. I was an adult but I was a kid again when I first got to college, just making my own fun if there was none, if you would have sat me down and tried to give the younger me some game, I would have blown you off and said "That's what's up." nodded

19

my head in agreement. "I'm going to meet my boys at the Caf, but thanks for the advice.", I guess. I would've responded exactly like that fighter that's cruising to a unanimous decision beatdown loss after just trying to survive for twelve rounds silently defying the pleadings of his corner. Now the funny thing about wisdom is you can't rush it, some things only come with experience, meaning if you're smart, after you screw up enough, you will learn from your youthful mistakes. You know that whole thing about "Youth being wasted on the young". well when you're young you lack the foresight and the experience to do better, which unfortunately when it comes to life is kind of like an unwritten rule. You have to get hit with a few punches that a savvy vet would've seen coming to learn a few lessons. Experience being the best teacher, right? As I rattle off another cliché that would make any young head strong kid roll their eyes in annoyance. Truthfully the prideful me is rolling his eyes as I write this, but I have enough wisdom, bumps, and bruises to know better. But now just as a bit of my undying youthfully defiant nature bubbles to the surface, that whole youth being wasted on the young thing, I say in response, wisdom is wasted on the old and weary and I'd give a very big middle finger to the mistakes that helped me write this book.

The Caf by the way, that was the spot, any good story of a gang of friends, band of brothers needs an origin, a common stomping ground where we all converged, the Caf was it for us. When I sat down to write this, I really gave it some thought, this is kind of where my story really took off. The boxing that kept us together years later would shortly come after but the Caf is where we all came together, where all the personalities came together to be specific. The food wasn't the best, I mean at first unlimited burgers, fries, and pizza sounds great.... at first. No what made the Caf special is that it was the social hub of the whole campus, minus classes or "The Set" on Fridays, everyone had to eat and the Caf was the place. That girl you saw that was the finest you've ever seen, right up until you saw the most beautiful woman on campus in the library a few hours later who could put the "It girl" from high school to shame, when you walked into the Caf she was in there, man to be real if you were in there long enough they both would be in there. The Caf is where it happened, from arguments about the last Madden game, political debates, to the hilarious misfortune of you being the next subject of that evening's joke session, and most especially, when your boy was finally able to show you the girl he had been lusting over for months because just then she walked in the Caf.

Oh and no worries about the argument, we can save that for later, so no need to get too distracted with what happened between my wife and I, I got this I'll get that shit straightened out, just you wait. But anyways the Caf is where we got together but this wouldn't be where I first met Theo or "TJ" as close family and friends called him, no I had known him years prior to our reconnection in college, but we were away from home and on our own now so things were different and by different I mean fun as hell. Now TJ was goofy as they get by nature, until this day he's probably the biggest kid I know or will ever know for that matter. He was the type of person to pull a prank in the dorms and he always got away clean. He was the orchestrator, but when things got real and people got pissed somehow they were never mad at him, on the other hand you never really saw him mad either, not to say he didn't have his moments but he was typically just the biggest kid among us and most people managed never to get offended or pissed off, strong emphasis on most people. See initially when we got to campus there was about ten of us, we stayed in the same dorm we all played Madden, so it was easy for us to gravitate towards one another. For those who don't know what Madden is, it's a very popular football game. It's the football video game to play. A few women play but for the most part it's a guy thing that many women get annoyed with because it takes up so much of their man's free time. Ladies I will say this, if he's playing the game that means he's home so cut him some slack. Madden is what we had in common, but after a few fights and just a natural realization that proximity doesn't always produce the best of friends, that ten would become four, but until then all ten of us would normally meet at the Caf. TJ is truly the fun-loving kid of the bunch, never letting a moment to joke escape all while never losing his temper or offending anyone, but nobody's perfect.

So it's homecoming and one of the guys in our group decides that it's a good idea that night to slap TJ upside the head as a joke, now if I can set the scene for you, TJ is about six foot with a decent bit of size on him, he has a low cut bald fade, so when the guy hits him in the back of his head, the loud smack we heard while walking from a vendor on a very cool October evening in Tallahassee probably added to the rage I saw in his eyes, as our friend not knowing what he had truly done strolled along, bouncing around in the best of moods, well until we had to hold TJ back. Now, you'd think this guy would have learned his lesson, TJ quickly reverted back into character smiled and said, "Hey it's cool bruh just don't do that shit no more". End of the story right, well not quite, a few weeks later we're gathered in the pavilion, we're down there just watching TV socializing with a few girls from the dorm and this guy again walks by playfully and "Pop! Pop!" he does it again! This time TJ has a certain calm look on his face, nods his head with a grin or a grimace I really couldn't tell, but he doesn't do a thing, I wouldn't understand why until that night. So later that evening we're piled up in the room playing madden ten people deep crammed in a tiny dorm room sitting on beanbags, desk chairs the bed, floor wherever we could sit. It's a typical night for us in the beginning, all seemingly had been forgiven and forgotten, that's until let's call him Sam for the sake of this story, silly ass Sam the disrespectful head smacking bandit decides to leave while we are in his room playing Madden to take a shower, no big deal right? Well remember that thing about TJ being a big prankster, well for those of you who haven't had a taste of college dorm life, you will usually find communal showers, disgusting showers particularly if you're in an all guy dorm, like the ones we happened to be in. That means when you went to go take a shower you leave your room, go across the hall, hopefully in your shower shoes (some of y'all were just nasty), sit your room key down on the bench outside of the shower along with your towel next to the clothing you wore in the trip over there right next to the clothes you're wearing when you came back fresh from the shower. In this case when you're Sam and you do that and you leave TJ in your room well this happens; while we're all still piled up in the room playing Madden, TJ sits there long enough to make sure Sam is in the shower, he quietly leaves the room and comes back with all of Sam's stuff; dirty drawls, clean drawls, shirt, shorts, towel, keys to the room and all, then locks the door, at that time nobody was paying him any attention. About two minutes there's banging at the door "Boom! Boom! Boom! "Hey man this shit aint funny give me my fucking clothes!" We look around confused then TJ says calmly as somebody gets ready to open the door "Don't open that shit". At this point we realize what's going on and TJ out of curiosity says, "What the hell is this man wearing", so he gets up and looks through the peephole in the door and falls out laughing, "Oh shit, y'all this man has on the nasty ass shower curtain!" When I mentioned earlier how nasty our communal bathrooms were, the shower curtains were included, you did everything you could to not touch them. I don't know whether those stains were from dirty water or mildew or what, but just imagine a large thick cream colored vinyl shower curtain speckled with stains and none of them being the same color which bothered me most, you never quite knew what they were so you did everything you could not to let the inside of the curtain touch your bare skin, and Sam nasty ass was wearing it. If it was a toga party, he was in dress code. Sam's pleading to open the door ranged from the initial anger to desperation, "Open the door come on man, dawg open my door!" back to anger, "Open my fucking door bruh "Boom! Boom! Boom! Boom! TJ was unphased, until his anger went back to desperate pleading one last time, Sam seeking sympathy said, "Come on man please, I'm itching!" which sent me, TJ, and the whole room into uncontrollable laughter. Sam had to be defeated at this point he had no phone, no way to do anything, all his friends were in the room and I doubt any of the other guys in our dorm were going to let a naked man in their room, well at least not wearing that petri dish of a shower curtain, but just when things couldn't get any worse TJ called the same girls that were in the pavilion when Sam felt brave enough to slap him upside the head for the second time, to come to Sam's room. We knew they arrived when we heard their laughter and the "Oh my god that's disgusting!", they also knew how disgusting the shower curtains were, I'm starting to think the girls weren't much cleaner. To make things worse they were taking photos of him with their phones and sending us pictures while he was stuck in the hallway, mind you we were still playing his PlayStation, this was between Sam and TJ, no need to stop the game and plus we all felt like he deserved it. So, when things settled and I guess TJ finally felt sorry enough for him or he just wasn't amused anymore, he unlocked the door and let Sam back in his room, which to me I thought ended the issue. Sam was going to get mad, kick everyone out and we'd just move the Madden night to someone else's room. Wrong again I was, I don't exactly know what Sam was thinking, but trying to fight someone while holding up a shower curtain isn't exactly the wisest thing to do as we all found out that night. It's one of those things where you must really want to and be ready to fight because at that point, you're either throwing punches butt ass naked or not at all, there's really no middle ground, someone should have told Sam that. Sam rushes in one hand on the shower curtain one hand cocked ready for action, he almost looked like an angry mother rushing out of the shower ready to start fussing, all he was missing was the shower cap. In an instant you see Sam being choked out with one hand, him on his back pinned between the bed and the wall. After exchanging expletives the thing I remember most is TJ saying "I'm a let yo ass up, you good Mufucka, you straight?" with firm grip still on that nasty ass shower curtain Sam says the only thing he can say, "Yea bro let me up". Then he proceeds to kicking everyone out, "Man y'all cut that shit off and get out since y'all wanna sit there and think shit funny", we left but not before ZO as we call him had to throw some salt in the wound. "Damn bruh, had yo ass hemmed up all in the nasty ass shower curtain, gosh damn boy! Got you going to the clinic and you ain't even get no ass, you caught them hands then a STD bout that shower curtain bruh, bahahaha, it's cool y'all we can play in my room." Really there was no need for that, but that was ZO for you, always had to get the last word, every fight was his and every argument justified, just the most argumentative ass if I ever knew one, but you couldn't find a better friend. He was complicated like that. He was the most caring, insensitive, sensitive, fun-loving, angry, peaceful, combative, humble, shit talker you'll ever meet. ZO a Haitian from Miami not in the roughest part but not from a place of affluence either, that undoubtedly had to factor in his personality and the way he was when he got mad.   Zaire, ZO's government name, he was caught between being a socially aware college student and a hard head from Miami, at times it was easy to mistake his passion for anger and sometimes they were one in the same, which always made for the most volatile but entertaining of arguments. His passion made him a great friend, but I swear this guy could get in an argument with anyone about anything. I remember introducing him to a friend of mine I haven't seen in a while from high school. Within about an hour these two dumb asses were about to fight over an argument about whether or not IHOP sold syrup in stores and if they did when they started, now knowing ZO I can't blame anyone but myself I already knew I couldn't take this motherfucker anywhere let alone to meet new people. It wasn't always like this, there was an entertaining side of ZO, one of those times happen to be an argument, it started in the Caf about Madden, it was all in good fun but anybody who plays madden knows that an argument in madden is not one of theory but one of provable fact, for us it was nothing but a walk across Wanish Way, the street between the Caf and our dorm to go hop on the sticks to make this provable theory a proved fact. So that's what ZO did. ZO was convinced he could beat this guy in Madden to the point he would let him pick his team for him. ZO was a good shit talker but he's humble by his own account, for some reason we weren't piled ten deep in ZO's room it was just ZO me and the guy. Sorry I'm about to take you on a detour but it's all important to the story. The guy ended up picking the New York Jets for ZO, not a horrible team but not a great one, I guess the guy had some sense of pride. The New York Jets that year had acquired a tight end by the name of Doug Jolley, I promise this is important to the story. The guy picks his team and the game starts, it's an ok game at first but ZO starts winning and then he starts winning big, now from the start ZO was talking trash he was running his mouth the whole time. "Oh, the Jets, oh ok, just know I'm bout to bust yo ass wit' these sorry ass Jets, you know why? Cause you a scrub! Scrub! Wit' yo scrub ass." The guy responds, "Ok we gon see", now at this point I can see he's already agitated with ZO, so by the time the game turns into a blowout the guy is completely silent, and ZO won't shut up. Then this happens, ZO's scores one last touchdown just to rub it in with that tight end Doug Jolley I was referring to before, during which he repeatedly as loud as he could ask the guy "You know why they call em' Doug!?" the guy stays silent, "Hey! Motherfucker you know why they call him Doug!?" after about the fifth time of him asking I'm wondering why myself,

I'm pretty sure the guy was wondering why too. "Because he just dug in that ass! Boooooooooooooy!". In mid laughter I look up and see the guy rolling up his controller with his eyes watering up, he mumbles "Fuck y'all" and leaves the room. Everyone is built different and I guess everyone has their limits to trash talking, by the way, if you were wondering, yes, that was one of the ten that didn't make it to four like Sam. ZO has almost gotten under all of our skin at some point, I mean close friends and family can do that, but I promise you this he's my brother but I would whoop ZO's ass before I ever let him run his mouth enough to make me cry like that but that's just me. ZO couldn't get under everyone's skin like that, like our boy Marcus. Marcus was just a cool customer, funny as hell and as easy going as they get. Marcus wasn't a big kid like TJ, he carried himself different, he was just a comedian at heart, and as southern as it gets, it was never really what he said all the time, but more of how he delivered it, he was always cool like that, you had to work hard to piss him off and even then he would make you laugh and diffuse the situation, it was just a natural thing he had. Marcus also had another thing, he loved the ladies; he wasn't exactly a "playa" or a womanizer, but he wasn't hurting for company of the female persuasion either. He always shot his shot, he wasn't always successful, but it wasn't for lack of an attempt. I recall plenty of times this exact scenario, Marcus: Hey hold up where you going with all that, lemme hold something. Random female: Excuse me? Marcus: Nah I'm just playing lemme talk to you for a minute. Random female: Boy bye! I remember a situation I even thought to defend Marcus, he was shut down so abruptly, he approached a group of women and in my opinion it was a relatively mild manner for his standards, but I guess not to them, they shut him down before he even got started. I began to say something, Marcus quickly stopped me and said "Nah bruh it's all good women do me like that sometimes, it's just me, it ain't nothing my boy?" Marcus was always cool; I remember he was so cool one night he scared the shit out of me. It was a cold night in late January we had all been back from Christmas break for about a week. At about one or two in the morning I go downstairs to my car to get something, what it was I have no clue, but I was expecting to be alone. I'm walking and I look up, I get startled I see something, something is moving back and forth, just rocking like something crazy out of a horror film. It's late, it's dark there's nothing but oak trees, the wind howling, and a few orange streetlights that really don't do much for vision at night but make for one hell of a shadow. "Shit man nobody knows I'm out here, that's how the monster gets you in horror movies, that's how they get the first guy to jump off the whole shit", that's what I'm thinking as I approach this figure. I'm running through the possibilities in my head, I recognize the heavy low lying branches swaying in the wind I recognize that but damn what the hell is this, as I walked closer my heart's beating faster, I can finally make out what seems to be a person, I began to relax in my head I say to myself " shit ok cool it's prolly a crackhead or someone who's mentally ill, yeah it's a crazy person either way they better mind they own business", because unbeknownst to them at this point they had just scared the shit out of me, " this one ass whooping they don't want tonight", I'm tough again right ? One on one I'm ok, monster Freddy Kreuger, Jason shit, hell nah, nope! So of course, wanting them to mind their own business I do what any normal person does, I walk by to make sure I can get a good look at who it is and make eye contact but he has on a hoodie so I can't fully see his face. As I witness this shivering weirdo close up I come to the conclusion, nope it's definitely a crazy homeless guy, so in passing I say what's up just to make sure he's friendly and when I get an even better look, I realize it's dammit Marcus! He was out here freezing.

Me: Yo' what up, you good man?

Marcus: Teeth chattering. *Oh yeah, yeah, I'm good bruh?* (He's not making eye contact anymore he's looking past me.)

Me: Dawg the hell you doing?

Marcus: *Just chilling.*

None of that shit sounded right to me he was being real short something was up and just as I look back for the second time to see what had him so distracted, it wasn't mental illness, it wasn't some drug induced behavior it was something much more addictive that mimicked the same actions as a victim of drug addiction looking for a "fix". He was waiting on Leah, who later would become much more than the Harriet Tubman of the girl's dorm that night, signaling safe passage to her room. See we were in college, but we didn't have coed dorms and if you got caught up there you got fined, how much I don't know because we never got caught, really, I don't know anyone who did.

Me: Oh, hahaha shit, ok my bad.

Marcus: *Yea, yea.*

He was a man on a mission but that was Marcus though, the four of us wouldn't be complete without him, but he was always good for a solo mission, falling off the face of the earth for days at a time, on a clandestine like operations with a girl that could rival a CIA agent disappearing act. It was always "Hey y'all seen Marcus? nah I ain't seen em all day or yesterday to think about it, not since we had lunch at the Caf. Y'all hit em up? Shit yeah I did but he aint pick up." That was a typical conversation about Marcus, he was always a man on a solo mission, but I understood those all too well, I wasn't pulling disappearing acts like Marcus all the time, but I had my moments. I think that's where it all went wrong, here we are just having fun in college then relationships get introduced. I won't ever make it seem like women or men are the problem it's a mutual thing, two young adults that have led separate lives, two different ways of doing things, different tastes in food, different perspectives and desires get together and it's supposed to work because of one overriding factor, attraction, hell at that age we don't even know who we are. When you're young let's not pretend we were resolute in our desire to have someone with great credit or someone that would be a great father or mother to our future kids, especially when you first go off to college that's the last thing most people are thinking about, as it should be. We're all happy to be away from home and have all the college fun we see in the movies. As for me, well I got to college and the older wiser me wonders what the hell I could have been thinking. I came to college with a girlfriend much like ZO did. I found out, like most people, college can be a place where you really find out who you are and who you're not. The Madden nights were great the club nights were even more fun, but I would find out that the allure and the trappings of a relationship will always catch you, even if you get out of one it's inevitable, we want that companionship but when you're young, you're doing it all wrong. I grew up heavily in the church and coming from high school I had a typical experience, well what I would assume is a typical experience, played a couple of sports, went to prom, and then I graduated. Bright-eyed and bushy-tailed off to college in my newly found relationship I had no clue this would be the first time I would break somebody's heart, I don't think we ever know before we do it especially at eighteen or nineteen years old, we have the most unrealistic expectations. I could best explain it like this, imagine a brand new young hungry fighter on the rise, you have all the hopes and dreams of being a legendary champion, then you get your first fight, you own the night, you get on a winning streak, you build a name, you have no thought of the devastation and the danger that you may encounter, you're young ambitious and ready for the world, you never think you're going to break somebody's heart, like how Manny Pacquaio broke my heart one December night when Juan Manuel Marquez came out of nowhere and flattened him in the sixth round. Boxing is a little different than most sports, the first time a guy loses or suffers a devastating loss you may never see that same guy again, some much hangs on every fight, so when you give somebody the ability to break your heart or claim a guy as "your fighter" a person can't help but feel devastated when it happens. For true fans when your fighter loses it's heartbreak every time. I've watched all of my friends go through it, being a fan of a fighter is truly like being in a relationship, you're watching each prospect looking for that fighter that's going to be the one, the fighter that looks like he has "It", a fighter you can have faith in, trustworthy enough not to let you down when it matters most. When you first get into the sport it's hard identifying those fighters who have those ultimate fatal flaws in their game that will leave you with the look of sadness and disappointment on your face after that first big loss, it's the sad face you haven't had since you were a kid when "Santa" forgot to get you the one thing you wanted most. So young and inexperienced with the world figured out already, something in a person catches our eye, we like certain qualities in people and without much contemplation we just go with it, we get better at it after our hearts get broken a few times, we watch with a more mindful eye, like yeah he looks good but I've seen that before you say to yourself, he holds his hands too low, great offense, no defense he'll get a dose of reality soon, I'll watch but I won't put my heart into it, you're dismissive, " Yeah he or she's a nice little fighter", but they don't have "It", that's not my fighter. The point of telling yourself this is you're not falling for that again; you're going to know the real deal when you see it next time. We all get skeptical like that after a few bad relationships, but there's one major difference between boxing and love and it's this, in boxing there are rules you must obey but in love, you just got to figure that shit out because the rules are............. there are no rules, so you're left to figure it out, weighing the advice of others in hopes of protecting yourself, much like I had to do when I found myself away in college with a girlfriend back home, surrounded by a sea of women.

Chapter II

It was inevitable.

I remember the first time seeing some of my favorite fighters. The first time they wow you, you get hooked, you can't wait to watch them again and in the meantime there's all the publicity and the build up to their next fight, then they live up to expectations or the truly great ones surpass those expectations, you get the feeling it could last forever, nobody's thinking about the end. Years pass and before you know it, they're not old but you hear rumblings of them slowing down and then of course some commentator gives them the kiss of death and says, "Father time is undefeated". "They don't know what they're talking about." you say, this love affair ain't ending anytime soon, now no fight fan says that part but that's what it is. You're saying he still got it, that's my fighter you're thinking. You're blinded by your affection; I remember watching Roy Jones Jr. not be Roy anymore. I was left thinking to myself how did this happen, he can recover, this is Roy Jones Jr. I rationalized his first true loss against Antonio Tarver, oh it was a lucky punch, Tarver had his eyes closed, the ten count was too fast and as the losses mounted, then I began to really realize how much time has passed since the first time I witnessed the greatness of a fighter like Roy, and damn does time fly when you're having fun. It's inevitable father time is undefeated, and damn ain't that the truth. I would always ask my pops when I was younger, why do we have to get old. It was a question coming from my fear of death as a kid, naively thinking only old people died. He would always respond "well it's better than the alternative". There's wisdom in that. I know now. Dead people don't age, it took me a while to understand it. It also took me a while to understand that there's a natural arc to life, you can't avoid it, you mature you get older and hopefully wiser. At first you're in college, you're an "adult", you have a girlfriend from back home it's going to work out with her, everything is supposed to work a certain way, the way you have it planned, you're young but you're smart, you know exactly what you're doing, there might be tough roads ahead but this is me, I got it, I got this! I bet every fighter tells himself that going into a fight before he realizes "oh shit I don't got it". The summer before I left for school, I met someone, call it a summer love. We were working as camp counselors. The relationship was new and who doesn't like new things, I'm of the opinion that the brand new feeling in life or the feeling of something new is the best feeling a person can have, it's a natural high, brand new in most people's mind brings new opportunity, new hopes, expectations, and a true sense of optimism even in some of the most hardened cynics. A new outfit, new sneakers, new car, anything. You get a new car and all of a sudden you're a new person, you put the good gas in it like you got money, you're worried about your mileage now, you used to be the first one to volunteer to drive for a road trip now you're hesitant, can't nobody eat in yo' car, you watching the way people get in, it makes you brand new for a while. You start acting like Eddie Murphy in *Trading Places* when he finally got on. We just love that brand-new feeling, just look at New Years and all the new year new me post on social media. That new feeling was precisely the reason why Elana and I were spending entirely too much time together, also I was leaving, so the sense of urgency was heightened. I remember the promises we made, they held up for a while. One of the biggest promises was that we would always visit. I remember riding that dirty ass bus for hours going to see her like every other weekend for the first six months. I was home it seemed just as often as I was in Tallahassee. She came to visit too, but it was nice to be back around familiar surroundings, also I liked not being subjected to communal bathrooms all the time. I would come into town and my parents wouldn't even know it. I was deep in the game, that summer love carried over into the fall, eventually winter and limped its way into spring. Meanwhile ZO and his high school sweetheart were doing the same but to the best of her knowledge Kayla believed they were skipping along without any issues, but ZO on the other hand ran into some "technical difficulties" a little earlier than I did in between Kayla's visits. ZO had secretly met someone, and it just so happens her name was Leah. This Leah looked eerily similar to the same girl that was signaling Marcus to make his way over to the girls dorm room the night he scared the shit out of me, because it was, imagine how crazy this is as I'm finding out from ZO as he describes in detail the girl he had in his room a few nights before. They didn't have sex but if I was her boyfriend I would have been pissed. See as a group we had no clue what Marcus was up to when he wasn't with us, to his credit he never really bragged. He was always dipping off without much notice or information, none of us had any idea that he had been talking to Leah, all but me and that was by accident, also none of my business. Women and men lie equally but this was on Leah not revealing that she was involved with Marcus to ZO, we would find out later, she lied to him because she was pissed off at Marcus. In between visits ZO had his fun, but when Kayla and ZO were together you would think all was well in paradise, they appeared to be doing the long-distance high school sweetheart thing right. Kayla even visited ZO with her parents on occasion, but when issues arose later, did they ever. That was Kayla and ZO, really high highs and really low I don't see how they're going to make it lows. That was due mostly to ZO's passionate or angry ways aside from his cheating. Someone that's that ready for an argument may have been too much for anybody to tolerate over time. This would drag on for years until it didn't, just that abruptly but not before things got interesting, but back to me.

As Spring was approaching, we had been back to school for a while since Christmas break. I had a chance to reflect on my time at home when I was back in Tallahassee, it was a little different, the summer love had become my long-distance girlfriend. It had become more normal to see her occasionally, rather than having unlimited time together for weeks at a time. We were together, but it wasn't brand new anymore, she was all in, but I wasn't so sure, we exchanged the normal I love you, but something was off. While we called and texted it wasn't the same especially after I returned to school from break, a living breathing girl in your face in a class you need to study for was way more appealing than a phone conversation. When spring break came, I went back home like she wanted me to, on that same dirty ass bus again, but to be honest I didn't want to. I wanted to do spring break stuff, college shit, the stuff I had been doing the whole time while I was away. I was completely faithful the whole time believe it or not, but temptation puts you in a different state of mind, mix that with a little distance and well the inevitable happens. Things just seem to get old and father time is undefeated. Now in a relationship it's different right, you can rekindle a flame get the spark back when things get old, I've never successfully done it, but I've heard rumors. The thing is how much and for how long do you put someone else's feelings above your own. That's the thing about love, I believe all facets of love involve this one characteristic and that is how much of you are you willing to sacrifice, and in regards to romantic love, is that sacrifice something you're willing to make with the person your currently with. That's the dilemma I found myself in, there was a lot of fun to be had, how much was I willing to sacrifice of my "college experience" just to keep her happy, what about my happiness, honestly what would make me happy? This woman loves me and she's good to me, I enjoy my time when I'm around her, but I didn't feel like being with her was eventually what was going to make me most happy. So, I ended it, I made the call, she didn't take it well.

> Her: *Heeeeeeeeey, I was just thinking about calling you, see we're connected, we miss each other. You miss me? When you coming to see me boy, you know I miss yo' big head ass.*

> Me: Bahahaha big head? Whatever, I miss yo' ugly ass too.

> Her: *Yes yo' big head ass, and I ain't ugly, you must be thinking about ya' other hoes. Hahahahaha.*

> Me: Hahahaha whatever, what you doing wit yo' silly self?

> Her: *Nothing bout to leave the house and get me something to eat, I don't know what I want but I'm feeling tacos, but I want some crab legs too I wish you were here.*

> Me: Shit get both.

> Her: *Boy I ain't bout to do that and all the good crab places closed anyway.*

> Me: Yeah you right.

Her: *What's up why you all dry tonight?*

Me: Nothing just tired…………... hey lemme ask you something, you happy?

I can't lie this is the part when you're trying to break up, you're hoping it's going to be easy like they have some hidden issues too, like the feelings mutual, you're both faking it, but a lot of times it just doesn't happen like that.

Her: *Yeah, why you ask me that? You happy?*

Me: I mean I am but………

Her: *But what?*

Me: I think the distance is a lot to ask for both of us, I'm young, and I'm thinking it might be good if we take some time off just to kinda make sure we know what we want.

Her: *You mean it's a lot to ask for you, I'm fine! What you mean, you serious right now?* Me: Look I'm saying………

Her: *Oh my god you're fucking serious! Where is this shit coming from? You talking bout you miss me, and now what? You trying to break up.......... You messing with somebody down there?*

As I began to explain myself, I guess reality sets in, I hear her breaking things in the background. No explanation I could provide would be good enough and at this point she wasn't hearing anything but heartbreak. As she begins crying it's apparent all fantasies of this being easy goes out the window immediately. I understand now that I look back on it, we weren't in the same type of love back then or maybe she was in love and I was just enjoying the moment until it wasn't that enjoyable anymore, I chose myself. Choosing yourself is a hard choice, well harder than it should be, it should be simple, right? Do what makes you happy, but it's not always easy especially when you're hurting someone, and she was hurt, angry all the above and she didn't mind letting me know either.

Now I have never been the biggest fan or critic of Fantasia, great voice and all, she's honestly alright with me, but my ex didn't do her any favors in the weeks following our breakup. For about two or three weeks straight she sent me Fantasia's song "Free Yourself", which I understood at first but damn every day for that long, I was just a kid now that I look back on it. I'm only eighteen some consideration should have been thrown my way she was ten years older than me, that's right, she was damn near thirty! See the allure of a grown woman that had her own place was too much for me to resist, it was great and technically being the teenager I was, not having to go home to my mom and pops but rather be with a woman who had her own place, car, money and no kids to speak of, the choice was too easy. In retrospect what the hell was I thinking, I know some women and even men reading this will ask what the hell was she thinking messing with that little boy, but we all make mistakes, and fellas let's not pretend if the right female who is of age, meaning an adult, comes our way we wouldn't hesitate to pounce, regardless of the age gap, it happens all the time, I just so happened to find me a cougar that's all. When I say what the hell was I thinking, I'm questioning my logic, going off to college seriously thinking about sacrificing my freedom while being surrounded by the largest, youngest, most ambitious, and talented group of women I would ever be around. Foregoing some of the best years of my life, man, I was what the old heads call a "new fool". I was a fool because freedom is hard to come by as we get older, that's the wisdom I learned on my own like every other teenager transitioning into being an adult had to. We just can't wait to get out of our parent's clutches to get released into the world so we can live the best life ever without any of the troubles and restraints that being a child brings, we're going to do it so much better than our parents did, we got this. Damn, when it's time to pay bills I wish I could go back, nobody ever told me the bills don't stop, I mean they did but they ain't tell me it was like this, I guess some things you have to learn the hard way. To be honest when I made the decision to let go of my relationship, I just wanted to be free like anyone wants, but I'm starting to think that free means in relationship talk, you just wanting to be tied down by somebody different than the old baggage currently weighing you down, because I ended up meeting someone.

TJ met someone too, well TJ met a few people, three to be exact, but I don't think he cares to bring up the first one much, so I will. TJ knew a girl from back home, Talacey, she came down to Tallahassee for school at the same time he did. I don't know the exact history between the two, but they never had any romantic interactions in high school from my understanding, but it's college, things change. TJ went on a few dates with Talacey early on, if I could best describe her all I could say is, she was bad, damn, like she brought back the Hallie Berry short haircut bad and simply for the fact she was live and in color she did it better in my opinion. We all thought so, just like TJ, which is why he was so ready to hand over his freedom so early in college. Talacey Berry on the other hand wasn't so ready. After a few dates we didn't hear much else, see he wasn't as secretive about things like Marcus was, he was proud, I would've been too. TJ didn't brag or anything, but he never hesitated to answer any questions regarding the situation. You and Talacey good? We asked while sitting around on a Madden night. He responded with less enthusiasm than usual. He explained that she wasn't ready to have a boyfriend and school was her priority, which could have been true but not likely, nobody in the room really said that but that's what we're all thinking. So y'all still hang out we asked? TJ: Yeah, we chill on campus sometimes and we got a class together. Which meant no we don't kick it like that anymore but to save face you have to play it out like that in front of your boys. ZO: Shit what she doing tonight? It's Saturday. Now ZO isn't a big instigator, but he damn sure dabbles in it from time to time. He asked that question knowing good and damn well that TJ would be out with her that night instead of playing Madden with us. TJ: She studying, I was trying to see if she wanted to go out to eat tonight, but she said she got an exam next week for chemistry. Ha! Chemistry, the very thing that was missing between TJ and Talacey. Marcus picking up on ZO's attempt to mess with TJ says, "Well shit my boy you might as well come with us to this block party shit we going to around the conuh' tonight." TJ: Yeah, I might. I can only imagine what was going through TJ's head, probably holding out hope that Talacey would send a text about meeting at the library or she would say you know what I am hungry, but we all kind of saw the writing on the wall. After a little convincing we finally got TJ out the dorm and dressed. As we walk across Monroe street you can already hear the music, it was a real block party, my first one. Not all ten of us went out that night but there was enough of us. We get to our destination; the block party was at these three-story multi-colored apartments. The front doors of the apartments faced out to the parking lot where all the action was. The front balconies on the second and third floor were one long walkway stretching across every door, it connected all the apartments on each floor along with steps at both ends for access leading up and down the first to third floor, so all anyone had to do to get a good birds eye view of the block party was post up and peer over the railings right outside their front door. So, when we got there, we made our way through the parking lot walked up the steps to the second floor where there were people standing outside with their cups having conversation looking over the railings, some were dancing, others were posted up with someone "special". We follow the music to one of the apartments on the second floor that had their door open, we saw the DJ in the middle of the apartment, with a good number of people doing more of the same of what we saw on the balcony, we stay for a while, a few of us found some girls to dance with but after a while the size of the party inside began to dwindle and the action in the parking lot started attracting more attention. We make our way out to the balcony and we find a spot overlooking the crowds that are growing larger downstairs by the minute. The largest crowd was centered around a group of guys showing off their motorcycles. One of the guys that had a bike that was royal blue and silver as I remember it, he kept revving the engine attracting our attention, of course curious females were circled around watching the main attractions, but one girl had the courage to hop on. The guy hands a girl in the crowd his helmet, we can't really see her, but I know at the time I was thinking "man this hoe really fell for that". That's me trying to pretend like I wouldn't have done the same thing the guy with the motorcycle did if I had the chance, ok so what we were hating, we all were. The motorcycle superstar hops on his bike and the girl climbs on the back with his helmet on that he had just given her, she holds onto his waist like a scene from a movie. They take a spin around the block and return to the very same spot where he and his other biker friends were, as they make their return the crowd watches and parts again like they did for them to get through when they left. It was like a scene from some nineties B Movie, where everyone is waiting for the leader of the biker gang to triumphantly return. The girl on the back of the motorcycle hops off and hands him the helmet, there are now three or four girls lined up just waiting for a chance to get a ride. They don't get a chance immediately, the girl lingers and now the guy is letting her take a turn revving the engine, attracting the same attention which initially attracted my attention in the beginning, I had turned away assuming ok next girl up once they slowly return navigating through the crowd. Then I hear one of the guys we are with yell out "Oh shit bruh ain't that Talacey?". "Damn that is Talacey!". I look and I'll be damned if it wasn't Talacey. I must admit in the moment we were all a little callous, I burst out laughing with the rest of the group. We were all laughing, all except for TJ and understandably so, she was supposed to be studying, she wasn't supposed to be going out that night. Reading this part, I know what some of you are saying "She could have changed her mind, she could have finished studying, she wasn't obligated to hang out with him when she was done, they're not even together.". All that is very true, but Damn! If the situation was reversed, he would seem like the worst guy ever and you do that to the wrong woman, your night would be a lot more adventurous than riding a motorcycle. See it wasn't that school was so important to her it was that he was so unimportant to even give a thought or a text once she had free time or she just straight up lied to him, either way public rejection is the worst. The look on T. J's face wasn't so much embarrassment although he had to be embarrassed, but just plain disappointment and hurt. Ladies your man is sensitive too he's unsure of himself too, that guy your talking to, seeming like he got "It" and he knows it, he's just as vulnerable and unsure of himself as you, maybe more, and he can be hurt a lot easier than you think, but he's going to do his best not to show it. Look at it this way, go back and listen to Muhammad Ali's post fight interviews or pre-fight build up, he talked like he was the greatest ever and he knew it, people hated him for his confidence. Come to find out one of my favorite quotes of his exposed Ali's very own self-doubt about his ascent to be the greatest of all time, "I am the greatest, I said I was great before I knew I was." See a lot of people understand that quote as Ali expressing his confidence in himself, but if there was a time he was unsure of his greatness, he didn't know if he was going to be great or truly how great he could be, there was doubt no matter how small, he was after all human, super human yes but a mortal man nonetheless with worries and self-doubt. That's in great contrast to the unflappable, unflinching nature of his boasts. So, imagine your man ladies or any man you engage with, chances are he ain't Ali, not even close. If Ali had his self-doubts you better believe any man you're dealing with is self-conscious to some degree and that's me putting it mildly, not to say he doesn't have confidence but he's not as sure of himself as he leads on. The same applies to women, women aren't without their pride, and vulnerability feels no better to a woman than it does to a man, men just might not be the best at handling it. With all that said I'm not in any way trying to make Talacey the bad guy in this, in her defense, she was just as young as we all were and she handled it the way a lot of people would have regardless of gender, she probably didn't know the best way to let him down, he was nice so it made it harder to be truthful, which seems backwards but when feelings get involved it makes sense for some reason. Nice guys don't always finish last, but they do finish last a lot. I will add this and this is not directed towards TJ but just men in general, fellas it's time we're honest, we have to stop using this "nice guy" thing as a way to guilt a woman to being with you and demonizing her when she needs more than nice. Imagine if as a man you were expected to accept any woman just because she was "nice". Look I'm going to tell you right now that shits not flying with me, that dog don't hunt, that shit don't cut the mustard and whatever other euphemism you can think of for hell nah, and I'm not ashamed to say it. Men fall in love with their eyes as many people believe, so it's just accepted that women should look a certain way, present herself a certain way to be suitable, which is fine I appreciate all you do ladies but men it cuts both ways. That's a double standard that I think is bullshit, I'm the furthest thing from a feminist but some of us are just lame and you need to step your game up, so when a woman chooses a guy who might have a little more baggage than you, maybe it's not her, maybe it's you, maybe you're too insecure, too fat, you talk too damn much and don't say the right things. Try hitting the gym, do some self-reflecting, be the man you would worry about your potential girlfriend or wife coming across and stop complaining. Sorry to get on my soapbox but I don't think that point is made enough, but back to TJ. I don't think TJ ever really questioned her about the situation, and now that I think about it, I never heard him mention her ever again, and we knew our limits we weren't going to ask anything else not even ZO. Talacey would later pop up with a boyfriend eventually falling off TJ's radar, but man that had to sting for a while. We all take losses, it happens.

So about that girl I met, it happened right before the year was over she had always been around she was friends with me and all the guys that we hung with but not the way some women are, " Oh I only have guy friends because I don't get along with other women". I hate when women say that, and it always makes me suspicious, you'll never hear a man say I don't have any guy friends, I only hang out with women. I believe women know a shiesty female when they meet one. Woman that's why they don't like you, they don't trust you. No, Camila was different she could hang with the guys and give them a run for their money she was' tough like that, but at the same time be just as feminine as any woman on campus and hang out with her girls, she was cool that way. You couldn't be "soft" dealing with her she was the type that would bring it to your chest, not by being disrespectful, but she definitely wasn't the quiet docile type, so when she took time out to hang with the guys, we all knew it wasn't that type of party. So, when I saw her and TJ hanging out it never passed through my mind that there was something going on, TJ never mentioned it and when I asked Camila, she said "TJ? No, we are just friends." Which made sense they played more like brother and sister than romantic interests. Camila and I got really close and before the summer I wouldn't say we were together but we were definitely in the courting phase, so much so that I found myself spending the night and when we woke up, well let's just say we both understood this was more than friendship. She stopped me before things went too far that morning, "No I can't be doing this, this is wrong". When she said that, I completely understood, she was not going to be the girl that I bragged about to all the guys that we hung around, I wasn't that type of guy but she didn't know that, and just in case I did say something, it would set a bad precedent. She wasn't having sex with anyone that morning. Camila was big on respect; she was as demanding as they got when it came to that. Directing any sort of rumor, bitch, hoe, type of name calling in her direction or approaching her about sex was the quickest way to get embarrassed and cursed out. See she understood one thing when you're young and immature a women's reputation is fragile with guys.

Summer break came and went and while she stayed in Tallahassee I went back home. Camila and I stayed in touch we talked about us; what the new year was going to bring we were both excited. So, when we finally got back it was strange that things didn't pick up right where they left off on the phone. TJ and the guys were at her place in between Madden nights we were no longer in dorms, she turned into something like a den mother, she would cook for all of us some nights, we even played Madden there a few times before she started fussing about how messy we were. We spent some nights together alone, nothing happened, I think we were really trying to get the spark back that happened before we left but we both knew something was different. Funny thing about communication there's so much to it; body language, tone, facial expressions, timing. That's why I used the analogy of boxing, the space and interactions between two fighters are so public but yet so intimate like a relationship, so with all the great advice in the world your corner may not be of any help, they aren't in your body no more than a friend giving you advice on what to do can be in your relationship or in your head. What we are seeing is not always what's happening. See when two people are involved in any intimate situation, if one or more of those components of communication are off in an exchange or interaction with a love interest, or someone who pays you close attention, then something just doesn't feel right. That's how most people get caught cheating, your habits are your weakness and you eventually get exposed when you're hiding something. See when you're so caught up being slick you never take into account the little things someone notices about you, the habits that you have developed over the years that you don't even notice, but they do, and after that any other differences in your behavior become glaring. One thing changed significantly. The guys came over less, but TJ was there more often, we were there at the same time sometimes, but he was there more frequently than I was. I would later find out that TJ had been to Tallahassee that summer and wouldn't you know it, low and behold she spent the night with him his last night in town. Of course, I didn't find this out from her, TJ became wise to the fact that Camila and I were closer than anyone knew, see on the surface Camila and TJ were the homie, friend thing, no lover involved, but from this experienced I've learned to "never judge a book by its cover" . Oh, if you haven't figured it out yet Camila was the second girl TJ met. But here was the problem, behind closed doors Camila and I had grown close so close that someone with a keen eye on one of us would notice. So once TJ figured it out, we talked one day in the gym and then I realized the extent to which they had been communicating. See a few months before that summer came, Camila asked TJ if they would ever be together, in a goofy moment TJ didn't take her seriously and said no as a joke. There was a third girl TJ never mentioned that had been hovering around this whole time so although TJ liked her, he never really felt compelled to explain himself, he figured it would work itself out, but a woman rejected had other plans. We never spoke to Camila about it, but we still came around like everything was normal, at this point she didn't know we knew, to be honest, not that it matters to her, until this day I still don't think she ever knew we knew. TJ had also figured out that there was another guy she had met that summer that neither of us knew anything about. See here's the thing about running a con on someone, you must be good at it, you can't get so caught up on taking advantage of the situation, you take for granted the intelligence of your "patsy". Camila lived with two other girls at the time in her apartment, they weren't friends just roommates that signed individual leases for their off-campus apartments. To make me jealous once I started giving her the cold shoulder, she tried to do petty stuff for attention, it never occurred to her that we knew what was up. TJ played it normal, he was stone cold, I guess she figured I was just jealous, she would do TJ's laundry fold his clothes at her house, make him whole meals, then make his plate, really go overboard right in front of me. So, I did want any man would do I sucked it up, I took my loss and I slept with her roommate. The look on her face the night she found out was priceless, it wasn't on purpose, I also had roommates and just one bathroom, so Camila's roommate invited me over saying I could use their shower, at this point, Melissa, her roommate, the two of us had been involved for a month or so without Camila knowing. Melissa had no clue that Camila and I had anything going on previously, whenever Camila and I spent time alone we were at my place, So she was really under the impression that TJ and Camila were a thing and I was just a friend he brought around when all the guys came over.

I remember taking a shower and like a dummy I didn't bring my own towels over. The way the bathroom was set up the towel closet was in the hallway. I yell out "Melissa! Hey, could you bring me a towel? I forgot mine." I had no idea Camila was home, well I knew it was a possibility, but her door was closed, and I couldn't see any light coming from under her door when I walked in, so I didn't know for sure nor did I care. Melissa brings me a towel and of course like any playful girlfriend she doesn't give me the towel right away, she plays keep away, we start laughing and making too much noise and I guess Camila recognizes my voice, so in the midst of me butt ass naked trying to secure the one towel that would cover me up Melissa hands it to me and she answers the bathroom door with an attitude. She opens up the door wide enough for Camila to see me just standing there in a towel, as Melissa says, "Sorry we so loud, we almost done, you need something?" she looks to be in shock and all Camila can say in that moment is "Oh. Really!?" she rushes back in her room and slams the door, I had some explaining to do with Melissa, but in my head, I was like "GOTCHA BITCH!". That had to be the most uncomfortable roommate situations especially on nights Camila walked in and I was in the kitchen. That pretty much ended the communication with Camila and I, but TJ wasn't done and why would he be, she was cooking and doing his laundry and to be honest he still liked her, she was cooking and cleaning for him partly to make me jealous but there was a large part of her that really liked TJ too, but she had been missing out on one of the most important things this whole time, well other than the fact we figured out what was going on, she didn't know about that third girl, who just so happened to be TJ's newly found girlfriend after he realized what she had been up to all this time. The only reason Camila didn't become suspicious of me or TJ was because TJ's demeanor never changed, see TJ's logic was the smartest thing to do is play dumb, "rope a dope" let her think she's getting the best of the situation. So, he did, letting her cook dinner for him, she was still doing his laundry. But slowly after each time he started leaving earlier and earlier to the point where he was just picking up his plate, his laundry, saying bye and leaving. She too inevitably stopped talking to TJ. After all that effort and lying she was gassed out and pissed off but wiser for it I hope, neither one of us ever spoke to her again.

Remember in the beginning I said that love can grow from almost any situation. Melissa was payback and TJ's girlfriend Ashley was something like a rebound, now we never openly admitted that, but it was what it was. Almost two years would pass, and these women weren't anything like payback or a rebound, well in my case that's true, I'll get to TJ later. I've only been in love with two women in my life and the crazy part is Melissa was one of those women, after explaining myself and getting over her initial anger we became best friends, partners, and everything else that comes with being in love. She was my college sweetheart. Things began to slow down, not time, just life, the group of ten became four, ZO, Marcus, TJ. and I. We focused on what was coming after undergrad more, and we played less Madden, but we picked up a new hobby, boxing. Well boxing wasn't new we had always talked about boxing but out of the group the four of us were the only ones that loved it and of the four of us ZO loved it more than anyone, see it went perfect with his nature, the guy that was always present for a confrontation. So, him loving a sport of pure unadulterated confrontation was natural. He was the type of guy that didn't mind going to the club on a Saturday night but would stay home and watch TV if there was a boxing match on without hesitation. ZO would choose boxing over any night in the club. For example, one night we all went out and he sat all alone on a Saturday night watching the Winky Wright vs. Sam Soliman fight. His love of the sport spurred our interest even more. We debated a lot and we debated boxing more and more as the Madden nights became less frequent, but a guy who's willing to sit at home and watch a boxing match while the world parties around him is the type of guy that always had the edge in a boxing debate, over time things would change as we went to the club less and hosted fight parties more. We were growing up and we didn't even know it. TJ had moved in with Ashley, Marcus and Leah got over their many break ups to make ups and the "friends" they had in between those periods, they were doing fine now. Kayla and ZO were still hanging in there. Melissa and I were great, but she was graduating and moving back home soon.

Chapter III

Touch gloves

Boxing became the lifeline of our brotherhood, as our relationships and responsibilities pulled us apart and time does what it always does, goes on. We even started boxing ourselves, as amateurs of course at a local boxing club, most of it consisted of sparring, conditioning the normal stuff, but we were participating in something we loved and the four of us were together. The Caf was a thing of the past, we had left behind the routine burgers, pizza, fries, and Madden debates and we didn't miss it. Every now and then we'd pop in for a trip down memory lane, but it just wasn't the same. Our meeting place now was either the local boxing club, someone's apartment for a fight, or a throwback Madden night once every blue moon. Ashley, TJ's girlfriend wasn't interested in boxing and she hated every time he hosted a fight. She especially hated when he left to watch a fight with us, but what could she do about it, but start an argument, which she did all the time when fight night came around. We all began to have issues in our relationships at some point. ZO and Kayla's arguments were the funniest and the most extreme, I remember one argument she suspected him of cheating, which he was but he wasn't going to admit to it. She went nuts on him right in front of us, they were arguing she was swinging cussing and fussing. She almost connected with a punch, that's when he was forced to grab her. She couldn't hit him, but she could keep cursing though. "You cheated on me I know you did you fuckin' liar, I hate yo' ass".

ZO: Stop jumping to conclusions you always do that shit.

Kayla: *No, this time I know, my friends said they saw you, why would they all lie.*

ZO: Really how many times have yo' friends said that shit? Huh?

Kayla: *So, you telling me they lying every fucking time? That don't make no sense. They said they saw your car next door at a girl's house that lives next door to one of their best friends and they said they saw you at her house!*

ZO's problem was his relationship was long distance, but she had friends that went to school where we were.

Kayla: *They know it was you, because you the only fucking dumbass with big rims and tints on a little ass fucking Kia hatchback.*

ZO: So, they saw my car what that mean?

This whole time mind you he's behind her holding her in a bear hug so she doesn't get loose and attack him.

Kayla: *You know what just let me go I'm done, I'm out of your life, just let me go so I can leave please*

ZO: Aight' fine fuck it imma' let you go.

Kayla: *Bitch then let me go then!*

ZO: Nah you too hyped right now, I don't trust that shit.

Kayla*: Let me fucking go!*

She tries one last time to get free by wiggling and stomping on his foot.

ZO: See that's the bullshit I'm talking bout.

In a much calmer demeanor seconds later she finally gives in and says, "Ok I'm good, I just wanna leave you and ya' dumbass friends let me go.................AND GET YO' DICK OFF ME!" ZO: Oh, oh, my bad. It was like she said the magic words, he finally let her go, she turns around winds up slaps him in the arm and with tears in her eyes she grabs her stuff and she was gone, not forever but she wouldn't visit for a while. I can't lie, men we do have a one-track mind sometimes, there she is pouring out her hurting heart and this man is copping a feel. TJ wasn't faring much better, he was coming over to watch the game a few weeks later, I forget who was playing but he was so late Marcus finally said, "Hey call this man and make sure old boy ain't laid up in no ditch or summin'." We call no answer, we quietly worry but we figure he and Ashely probably got something going on, and man did they. We hear a knock at the door, I answer, it was TJ as ZO assumed, I could tell something was off though, that goofy ass smile he usually has is nowhere to be found. ZO yells out just to start something "Bruh, you always late!" TJ doesn't respond with his normal shit talking, he just blurts out, "Man I almost beat this hoe ass".

ZO: *Damn bruh you good what happened?*

TJ: This fucking girl just spit in my face. (All of us in unison SHE WHAT!?)

71

ZO: *Bruh what you mean she spit like while y'all was arguing by accident?*

TJ: No bruh she straight up spit.

ZO: *What!? Oh no........................ Motherfucka you better than me that's all I'm a say.*

ZO: *Damn for what?* (Like it even mattered.)

TJ: Bruh you know how she get, especially when we get together so we started arguing I told her she can talk that shit to somebody else and she just went overboard this time, man I had to leave I saw myself whooping her ass. I had been left I just been riding around though. ZO says Damn! At this point it's nothing we could really say to him, for me personally I can't say for sure what I would have done, but I'm pretty sure my chivalrous ways may have escaped me in that moment. A few months later after TJ cooled down, he finally told me what all happened. Watching TJ interact with Ashley I could see how it went down after talking to him. Ashley's parents had a little bit of money and I guess being from the New York tri-state area, that attitude she had was built in, but her parents made her a brat. TJ was so goofy I would witness him in mid argument, he would shut down and go into little brother stop copying me mode and mock her just to get under her skin, especially if he felt like it was a pointless argument. He had his own way of remaining calm, he was playful, for as long as I've known him, I've heard people tell him he plays too much as many times as I've heard them say his name. I can't emphasize this point enough, if you didn't know how to speak English and you were around him long enough, you would think his name is "stop playing" last name "you play too much". This is the story as he tells it. *Bruh so you know how she gets when I'm hanging out with y'all or we just have a fight night at the house. That night she was on some different shit, so she tryna find stuff for me to do around the apartment to keep me at home long enough for me to just stay. So bruh I cook, 'cause her ass can't and then I tell her whatever she got going on I'll handle it when I get back. She goes off talking bout you don't do shit, you always with your boys' blah blah blah blah. Mind you bruh I just cooked, she spoiled as shit this the same girl that slapped her momma and her momma apologized. She a little spoiled brat bruh, her parents had a little bit of money and they spoiled her, so she used to getting her way.* There was a little delay but when it registered what TJ had just said, I stopped him.

Me: Whoa, whoa, whoa, nah bruh rewind, she what?

TJ: *Yea bruh, she told me that shit one day out of an attempt for sympathy when we first got together and talked about our families. She said that her mother punched her in the mouth, and I was like damn that's messed up right?*

Me: Right.

TJ: *So, after I get to know her, I asked her a few months later what happened with that because I got to know her crazy ass and I knew if anyone deserved to get punched in the mouth by they momma it was her ass. She told me back when she was younger like fourteen or fifteen, her momma bust in her room, telling her to clean up, I guess she had been telling her all day, so then she says her momma started throwing stuff off her bed telling her to clean up, so she finally starts cleaning, but Ashley say she starts ignoring her when her momma starts asking questions 'cause in her words she cleaning and she was already mad, her momma was just trying to get on her nerves. Then she say her momma comes up behind her yelling in her ear and she just turned around and slapped her out of reaction, then her momma punched her in the mouth.*

With a mixture of being shocked and entertained, I started laughing but I could see TJ's face he wasn't laughing he didn't find it funny right then, so I let him continue with his story.

> TJ: *Yea so I shoulda known then what I was dealing with, but yea so we start arguing but you know me I ain't one for the arguing shit especially if it ain't bout nothing, so I just start laughing and saying ok you right, you right and kept putting my shoes on, that's when she try to run up on me like she wanna square off, so I put my shoe down stand up, she flinch like she wanna swing, so I grab that wrist before she can get to my face, that's when that dirty motherfucka spit in my face.*

> Me: Damn, you ain't do nothing?

> TJ: *Hell, yea I was about to whoop her ass, I let her hand go to wipe the spit off and then I get in her face cussing her out, bruh I was ready to go to jail that night.*

> Me: Shit, I bet.

I can't lie she was dirty for doing that, but I was in between being entertained, being a friend to listen and imagining if I had made the wrong choice in that moment and having a record.

> TJ: *She got scared and tried to apologize but I just left and went driving 'cause the more she talked the more pissed off I got.*

I'm not going to speak too much on Ashley's actions, but I've heard this from my parents as many of you have, but ladies and gentlemen I'll say it again for those who missed this lesson, if a person can't respect the people who brought them into this world they'll never respect you. Here's a warning leave they ass alone it won't end well. Of course, in extreme situations where parents are absentee or abusive there are exceptions, but just be decent you don't have to love everybody but show them the basic level of respect. That's the thing about being a nice guy, Ashley tried that because she knew she had a "nice guy", but she pushed him to the point where he was ready to kick her ass, I know TJ and a woman beater is not in his character at all but that's what he would have been labeled if he reacted on his impulse. So, that was pretty much the end of Ashely and TJ, but it would take some time, living together then splitting up is nowhere near as easy as breaking up long distance over the phone, which is what Melissa and I wanted to avoid. We didn't want to be the typical long distant disappointment, so with one of the more painful romantic moments in my life we decided to end it, face to face when she graduated and left, see back home was just too much distance where she was from for us to really have a chance. We felt if we stayed together, we were setting ourselves up for failure. So, we ended it mutually. We had so much respect for each other, that we knew we would rather have a what if, rather than end on a sour note, we wanted to leave each other with good memories. In retrospect I don't know what would have been best, one of us letting each other down from a distance or letting go too soon. Marcus and Leah had their bumps in the road but out of all of us around this time they were doing ok, considering. My last year of undergrad we were all single well ZO and Kayla were still on and off but for the most part we were all single except for Marcus.

After some time, Melissa and I kept in contact, but she eventually met someone as did I. Maybe it was my readiness to be in a relationship at that point, it's always a weird time after a breakup. Things picked up quickly with Tarah and I, the new woman I met, the irony of it was she lived out of town a lot closer but still, I could only imagine what Melissa would say. I met her when I was back home visiting my parents on a random weekend, at the time she was a nurse that went back to school to become a nurse practitioner and I was about to graduate. Tarah and I weren't best friends starting out, but it didn't much matter because she was fine and compared to how Melissa and I started off, we were going to be ahead of the game. Damn! She was fine, so to be honest; it didn't matter much how we met. Tarah was the type of fine that makes a man forget he was in love just a few months ago, the type of fine that will make a man overlook fatal flaws that might come back and bite him in the ass. I wanted to be friends with her, but I wanted to be the type of friend she called on late at night, so that's why when I saw her, I had to take my shot. My lust was all I needed after Melissa, "I was gon' be alright!"

During this time of transition for all of us ZO would come up with his best idea yet, no matter where we were next year he wanted to go see his favorite fighter live in Las Vegas, Manny Pacquiao and we were all going, none of us at that point had been to Las Vegas, not for leisure anyway and definitely not for a fight. That's one thing ZO and I had in common, Manny Pacquiao, ZO loved him for his aggressiveness, I did as well but I also loved his approach, smiling every time he made his way to the ring and thrilling every time he stepped in it. We all liked Manny, so it was a no brainer. Little did we know at the time, ZO's idea to take this trip would start an almost 10-year tradition of our guys trip to Las Vegas for fight week. The planning and expectations for this trip was almost as fun as the actual trip itself. In between though some major changes were brewing. One day Marcus was at ZO's house and he had called TJ and I to come over. It was a weird day, no trash talking or video game playing, we were all just chilling, watching TV not really talking about anything now that I think about it. It felt strange, then out of nowhere Marcus announces "Aye y'all, ya boy heading to the Air Force". In shock we all kind of just said that's what's up. Dang it was happening, the realization that the team was breaking up was a little surreal. That was the big news, ZO had been the first to know. I guess at that time ZO finally felt comfortable to tell us his big news. Kayla and ZO had gotten back together and eloped, this man was dammit married for three months and none of us knew until now. So, I was up, to everyone's shock I had an announcement, I let everyone know that Tarah was six months pregnant. It was a convergence of coincidence, see life was doing what it normally does, ushering us into the next stage of adulthood without our consent. When I look at it now, it all made sense, the plan was always to graduate and move on at some point, but damn does time fly when you're having fun. We started together so our big news was right on time with life's schedule. TJ was still TJ, he made his jokes, he made light of everything, I guess it was to be expected, he was the only one without a major announcement, at that point he was just dating here and there. Marcus wasn't leaving until next year, so Las Vegas was still going to happen, as for the rest of us that were left, we planned to stay and attend grad school in town, but things wouldn't be the same once Marcus left.................................. Shit! I'm about to be a father.

Chapter IV: Part 1

Happy wife, happy life.

Some of us go quietly as age ushers us along through life others fight it tooth and nail. It's because you lose things as you get older, you lose hair, you can't help it, but you lose some of your optimism. I remember thinking that everything was going to work perfect, problems were only for people that caused them. When I was young, I couldn't imagine how people just got themselves into situations, I was too smart for that, I would learn later not to judge. You also lose time, that's a big one, especially when you look up and wonder where it all went. We all want more time, but the crazy part is the more fun your having, the busier you are, the quicker time moves. I never understood when someone would say "There's not enough time in the day". I always thought there was too much, too much time until the bell rung in high school, too much time until Christmas came, church was way too long. So, when I heard "There's not enough time in the day." I thought it was crazy. If I could sit down with my younger self, I would say don't even worry about pondering the how's and the why's, you will soon get it, it's an adult thing youngster you just wouldn't understand right now. On the other hand, when you're miserable or in a miserable situation time stands still even as an adult, like if you're at a job you hate, or you're stuck in a bad relationship or an even worse case a bad marriage. I remember when I was with Melissa, we were recalling that whole bathroom incident with Camila and to both of our surprise it had been over a year since that happened. Where did the time go? It's just life you can't stop it. Life is not without its balance though, you lose time, but you gain wisdom through your experiences. I was losing some of the freedom I enjoyed so much as an undergrad, but I was gaining a son. I was excited about the addition to my life I was going to be a father, but how the hell did this happen? That's my nervous side. I mean I know how it happened, of course but I was just in the Caf complaining about how tired I was of the burgers and fries yesterday or at the latest last year right? I would find myself going through my normal routine preparing for graduation or enjoying myself kicking it with my boys and it would hit me, I have a son on the way. The immature me back then was happy it was a boy, a girl would have made me worry instantly, well worry way more than I already was. I wouldn't call it a dark cloud looming over me because when I was planning the whole process with Tarah, things seemed like it would be ok, her calmness was reassuring, this was new territory for both of us but she was handling it like a G. Things definitely were changing, ZO was married and Kayla was moving in with him before he started attending grad school, he had a wife now, and it was Kayla. What!? They had come a long way from that argument a while back. See ZO's passion made him impulsive at times, he was ready for a fight, but he was also sensitive, I think he was just as ready to be the man who was caring and faithful as he was angry or passionate, but insecurity and pride can get in the way of the person we truly want to be. Sometimes we do things out of insecurity, we make decisions, selfish decisions to protect ourselves from getting hurt and make decisions that end up hurting other people, especially men, not making an excuse for his previous actions, I'm just explaining what I know as it pertains to him. During the time Kayla and ZO were apart, ZO was dating but he would openly admit Kayla was "It", constantly, "she was the one, nobody can compare dawg." "Man, I can't lie any girl coming after her is gonna have a hard time bruh." He said that like Kayla had it easy, sometimes you have to let your friends vent. I wanted to tell him ok bruh we got it, Kayla's the "one", but you were the one that ran her off. I will admit, he did get her back though. See the allure of marriage for a woman that is truly in love with a man, sometimes is too good to pass up, the idea of it is what I think she was in love with and ZO took advantage. I have no doubt she loved ZO, but to keep it real there are some things in life that are damn near impossible to make it back from. But what woman passes up her high school sweetheart, especially today, it just doesn't happen like that anymore it's a rarity and everyone wants to feel like their love is special and rare. Making a home, baby dolls, and family are not what little boys are taught or steered towards, so for guys wanting stability and family comes later, like after we have had enough "fun". That's not to say, it's not modeled by our fathers, it's just a different maturation process growing up to be a man as opposed to becoming a woman. So, ZO was able to sell her, see passion can appear to be anger but it can also be a tool of love that can mend the most broken of hearts, combine that with a big gesture like marriage and well game, set, and match.

There's a lot of selfishness in relationships I believe. I think people get caught up on the idea of keeping someone and not keeping them happy. I think if ZO would have been honest with himself back then, he would have admitted that he loved Kayla, but his pride, not just his heart wanted her back, but he wasn't ready to keep her happy.

Keeping someone happy requires sacrifice, compromise and ZO wasn't the most compromising individual. He demanded honesty but he wasn't so honest with her. While ZO was dating in between their time apart so was Kayla. I think ZO forgot women can lie too or maybe he thought his girl now wife was too good for that. One afternoon we were all at Marcus's place, but it was a bit augmented, the time with my boys that is, instead of it just being the guys Kayla was now here and Leah who would be around every now and then had become a staple since Kayla had moved to town, she now had someone to have "girl talk" when she was with Marcus and not a bunch of boxing arguments and video games to just sit there and witness. Tarah was back home, she was still in nurse practitioner school and she worked part time at the hospital she was interning at, so in the meantime she moved back in with her mother which really helped me while we were apart. TJ wasn't there yet like usual, ZO may have had a point, he was always late. We're playing games sitting around on a Sunday afternoon, it was a good day. ZO of course mentioned the fact that TJ was late, it was almost like normal, then he suggested we all go to the grocery store. Marcus didn't have any food and ZO wanted some juice. Hey bruh lets go to the store, I respond Why you

86

need all us to go to the store man? I'm in the middle of a game. "After the game I mean bruh, yo' ass losing anyway, let's go as a family" ZO says. I was losing as his bitch ass had to point out, even when ZO was being cheesy and nice, he talks shit. That "lets' go as a family" comment was cheesy, but I get it at this point we were like brothers, we are brothers. After some convincing I caved, I tried one last time to find a way out by pointing out that TJ wasn't here yet, but it didn't work. ZO: Just call that man, he always late we can leave his ass, just let him know we gon' be at the store" Marcus: Shit, y'all can go, imma just wait on my boy, I aint gon' leave em' like dat'. Marcus wasn't slick, his ass didn't feel like going either. ZO kept insisting, when he had his mind set on something that's just the way it was going to be or at the very least, he was going to make every effort, and going to the grocery store as "a family" is what he wanted. Marcus not being one for pointless debate responded "aite bo whatevers clever". Kayla and ZO head out to the car. Marcus and I linger finishing the game, Leah waits with us alongside Marcus as the game finishes. fifteen- or twenty-minutes pass. I was surprised ZO didn't bust in asking what was taking so long, so I got curious. I walked outside and I could see ZO and Kayla in an intense discussion, so I figured I'd let them be.

87

Marcus: What they doin', they ready? Me: Naw they talking about something out there. Marcus: Shit aight then, I'm a go upstairs for a minute I'll be back let me know when y'all boys ready. Marcus walks upstairs, I go to check to see if they're almost ready, just as I head to the door, ZO busts in. "Lying Ass Motherfucka!" Kayla comes in behind him, "I didn't lie, I told you I was talking to somebody before we got back together."

> ZO: No, the fuck you didn't! You said you went on a few motherfuckin' dates!!

> Kayla: *What do you think that means?*

ZO breaks it down.

> ZO: THAT! MEANS! When I was asking you, have you been messing with anybody you don't just say you been on a few fuckin' dates! FUCKING AND DATES ARE TWO DIFFERENT THINGS!!! (Nobody gets angry like ZO.)

> Kayla: *I mean did you really wanna know everything.* (She asks pleading her case.)

ZO: Yes, that's why I was fucking asking! (He didn't really want to know; he wanted the answer she gave him, and she knew it.)

Kayla: *Well I'm not a mind reader, I didn't know!*

Pause for a second everyone, she knew good and damn well what ZO meant when he was asked that, she was playing dumb I know that routine too well, I perfected it. Just as I get ready to sit down and get my popcorn ready to watch the show, ZO kind of has a sixth sense about the fact that Leah and I are about to become an audience with front row seats, and he leads Kayla outside. I try not to be nosey so I don't peak through the blinds, but I can still hear shouting. After a couple of minutes, I hear nothing. I assumed they drove off to handle the rest of their business, so I check outside making sure, thinking good, I don't have to go to the store now. I look out and I see ZO's car was still there, ZO's there but Kayla is nowhere to be found. So, I go outside to talk to him, leaving Leah on the couch and Marcus still upstairs, I'm pretty sure he's taking a shit at this point. Me: Everything good? ZO: Yea bruh just this lying ass female. Me: Where she at? She left? I'm only asking because they rode together, and it wasn't a short walk back to their place she would have had to have been really pissed off if she walked. ZO: Nah her stupid ass over at the bus stop across the street, I told her dumb ass the bus don't run on Sundays. Just then two guys riding by notice her at the bus stop and shouted out something from the car, I didn't notice because I had my back turned talking to ZO nor was it loud enough for either of us to make out what was said, but ZO saw them and he knew they said something to her. So, I hear him say hold on, after a second or two I turn to see where he was going, I don't think he ran but adrenaline does wonders to the human body. As I look back, I see ZO already has cleared the fence and was almost across the street sixty yards away when I turned around. I was like damn he got there fast, I assumed he was going for Kayla, but he went past her to the gas station. I wasn't going to follow him until I saw him go into the gas station. So, I made my way across the street thinking "What the hell is he mad at now?" Just then I see ZO and two other guys coming out of the gas station arguing, well he is arguing with one of them, but the guy with the dreads is silent. I'm confused at this point but then I hear the guy say, "I was just asking her if she needed a ride bruh, you better chill". Which set ZO off even more, so I try to diffuse the situation, but ZO was looking for a fight, I would find out later that the guy he was arguing with pulled a knife on ZO when he approached him in the gas station. I don't blame the guy, some stranger runs up on me, I would be on guard too especially assuming how ZO had probably approached him. I try to talk to the guy that seemed calm, two sensible people diffusing the situation, right? So, it starts off well, I say man he just got into an argument with his wife, he's just mad at everything right now, the guy says, "cool but get ya' boy". Dammit why couldn't he leave that last part out! Soon as he says that ZO hears him and tries to start arguing with the well-mannered, dreaded, sensible gentlemen that I was having a peaceful conversation with to diffuse the situation. Being the well-mannered sensible gentlemen that he was, he remains calm but then proceeds to throw up hand signals that I can only assume are gang signs and just as calmly he says, "It's ok we gon' get the heat." "What? I thought we just had a moment brother, no heat, it's Florida we already hot" that's what I was thinking as he gets into his car, thankfully he didn't have it on him at the time. So maybe he was bluffing, that's what I'm thinking as we cross the street heading back to the apartment. Yeah, he was bluffing if he had a gun and he was a gangster like that he would have had it on him he was bluffing. As we were heading back, we see TJ with his late ass at the apartment heading towards us, he "asked what happened, y'all boys straight?", he thought ZO and I had got into it which wasn't farfetched. I explain the situation as we go into the apartment all while ZO stupid ass is trying to defend is actions. I'm thinking like Craig from Friday when he and Smokey got into debt with big worm and couldn't pay up. "He know where yo' momma stay! My momma stay!". That was just the feeling I had, because they just clearly saw us walk back across the street to Marcus's apartment, but then I thought again, man they were bluffing they about to go on about their business. By that time Marcus was back downstairs and he and TJ were laughing at us about the situation. Oh, I'm the only one taking it seriously, ok, that's what I'm thinking, TJ heads to the kitchen, Kayla had come back and was in the living room with Leah. I sit back down and then I hear Marcus ask, "is that dem?" Shit it was them as I look out the living room window, they walked right by, they didn't know exactly where the apartment was. Damn, I didn't see a gun, but why would they come back if they didn't have one though? The girls were scared as shit they were quiet, I forgot they were even there. After Marcus and I convince ZO stupid ass not to go out there, like literally they can't find us they walked right by us, TJ volunteers to go speak to them. TJ the easy-going prankster that gets along with anybody is like man "I'll go talk to em'." TJ is out there for a while, so we head out there to check it out, TJ is coming back and said "y'all good, man they aint even worried about y'all." We look and it's not even the damn guys that we got into it with, I go talk to them and they say, "Shit they had a gun, so we pulled out our shit." Welp, then, it's settled we staying our ass in the house. Damn they did have a gun, so we all go in the house it's not funny anymore. One of the girls calls the cops, but not before ZO grabs a butcher knife and gets ready to go outside. "Man, what the fuck you doing I ask?" "Man, I ain't gon stay in the house scared like a bitch!", ZO says. This man was literally about to take a knife to a gunfight, I can't make this up. I was about to have a son and this man is trying to be the Haitian Rambo. You could be the toughest Haitian with a machete but in a gunfight, "Sit yo happy ass down!" as we instructed ZO, and it didn't take too much convincing, the only person bluffing I think at this point was ZO. The cops arrive and at this point I guess the guys had left, crisis averted, a day at the grocery store as "a family" never seemed so appealing. We ended up not going and just getting a pizza. I know I wasn't going anywhere. I had a family to think about, technically we all did, we're brothers, but ZO's anger blinded him to that. Shortly after that incident, that would be the end of ZO and Kayla. She had had enough, she moved back home that next week, I guess she told her parents everything and the simple dissolution of marriage papers were sent shortly after. ZO was crushed, he said "I don't get what I did that was so wrong, she can't even respond to an email bruh". He had the nerve to make an utterance about a year later after Kayla refused to communicate with him in any way, that she was wrong for cutting him off. She did cut him off "cold turkey" but I don't blame her, she didn't even let him know that she was never going to talk to him again she just didn't. When ZO asked what did he do so wrong, I was thinking what did you do right? He forgot the golden rule of marriage, "Happy wife, happy life".

I on the other hand, after I found out Tarah was pregnant, I was not planning on getting married, being a father was task enough for me. I need to make it clear; marriage was the furthest thing from my mind, Las Vegas, grad school that was the plan.

Chapter IV: Part 2

Happy wife, happy life………Right?

We are just taught certain things in life, excuse me, please and thank you, get a job, pay your bills, you get married then you have kids, when you're young and inexperienced you don't closely examine the how or the why behind it, you just do your best. At about four months into the pregnancy right before I broke the news to the guys Tarah hinted at not wanting to be a "baby momma". I'm just really grasping my future reality of becoming a father, I didn't ignore it, but it didn't quite register what she was getting at. See nobody was really in my ear about my situation because only my boys knew and we had our boundaries, we didn't really step into each other's business unless we were asked, family on the other hand was a different story. I hadn't yet broken the news to my family because I was a bit nervous about my parent's reaction, here I was ruining the prideful moment of their first and only son graduating from college. The way my family would see it; I was a young college graduate with nothing to hold me back and a child would severely hinder that. I manned up and eventually told them after I made the announcement to my boys, my pops was furious, I never thought he would be this mad, disappointed yes, but this mad? I remember him saying "Since you a big man and you starting a family, you can pay for your own damn phone and I shouldn't need to send you money right!?" My father and I have a great relationship, but he was a no-nonsense type of guy. It's crazy to think my grandfather was my father's father, they are polar opposites. My grandfather prevented me from getting plenty of ass whooping's at the hands of my pops as a kid. I would see my grandfather pull rank on my dad it was great, not to see them go back and forth about me, but to get saved from an ass whooping. My grandfather's response was completely different from my pops, he just simply asked "Well grandson what you gon' do?". It's the same question I asked Tarah when she first told me she was "late". She told me she didn't want to have it, but me being the dumbass I was, I naively convinced her that everything would be fine, we can have this baby, which I didn't know it at the time but that was putting one of the final nails in the coffin of my bachelorhood. See she was finishing Nurse Practitioner school at the end of the year, so I figured I'm graduating, she is going to have a great career, what's the big deal? My grandfather asked that question of what I was going to do with different motives, see one thing my pops and my grandfather did have in common is the church. I grew up in a religious household and it started with my grandpops, which is where I met TJ, in the church. My family was concerned about me having children out of wedlock, I hadn't really given it a second thought. The only thing I knew at that point was, I was going to graduate school, but even then, I hadn't truly thought about going to graduate school directly after I graduated. I was going to take some time out, work a job that was good enough and party, but my incoming son would change all that. I felt the pressure to be successful and when my family got wind of the new addition it just amplified the pressure. My father tells me it's time to man up, we have a conversation about getting married in which I reveal some of the talks that Tarah and I have had, he then lets me know she was dropping major hints about getting married, shit it all made sense, that "I don't want to be a baby momma" comment wasn't just about an abortion, it was about getting married, it was the preamble to an ultimatum that inevitably would have come. It never really came down to that though, because after some "convincing" from my father, I decided I was going to propose. My grandpops, my pops and I go to the mall to find an engagement ring. I love my pops, he wanted the best for me, and now when I think about that time it makes me smile, three men figuring out this part of life together, this was uncharted territory for my grandfather as a grandparent and my pops as a parent, and me as a man, for my grandfather there was no ass whooping to talk my father out of giving me this time, or allowing me to eat a piece of candy my mom and pops said I couldn't have, this was more serious, for my father it was time to show me the "right thing" to do as a man, but with all the guidance and advice I would get, they neglected to fully explain how hard marriage really would be. So, I ask Tarah out on a date and I do it, after dinner we go on a walk downtown, I drop down to one knee, I man up and I ask her to marry me. She of course says yes. So, there I was twenty-three years old engaged in January, set to be married in February, a baby in April, graduating later that April and oh yeah, Las Vegas in May. Life was coming fast. See my family and my fiancé' pushed for us to be married before the baby got here, a classic "shotgun wedding". I know it looked good on paper, but it wasn't the wisest decision in retrospect. End of February comes and we just have a small wedding on the beach with my wife to be at seven months and really showing, my boys weren't there, we would always say a man can't go hunting without his dogs but this wasn't that, the hunt was over and I had been the prey, everyone was having a luau and I was the pig with a skewer in his ass. It wasn't a big event, no huge party just a small collection of family, a mixture of hers and mine with my grandfather and my pops being my best men. It was more like a small get-together. It wasn't perfect but I'm starting to realize at this point earlier than most, life isn't always perfect, so I really was happy at the time. Here I was a brand-new husband, about to be a brand-new father to a baby boy, brand new college graduate and let's not forget, Las Vegas. That brand-new feeling had me on cloud nine. I was a new man I had a wife and a family, there was only one problem, none of this shit came with any instructions. You get a new car there's a manual, new tv there's a manual, well the tv doesn't matter no man reads the instructions to a new tv anyway, but you get my point. The end of March, Tarah moves in with me in Tallahassee, it's real, now I'm her full time caretaker, she had graduated from NP school back in December right before her 26th birthday earlier that month, so it had been a busy time for both of us from November until the time she moved in, in March. Things were hectic and the baby wasn't even here yet, but March was moving like it had somewhere to be, I blinked.

Baby's here! April comes and I'm a father, no lie the absolute greatest day of my life and it gets better graduation is a mere three weeks away. I'm a college graduate guys!!! There was just this buzz of newness in the air you could feel it. I'm a grown man now, no time for childish games, I have a family to feed, my wife was going to stay home and take care of our son and I was going to make it work. We would get occasional support from our family, but this was my family and I had it under control, but there was one small issue. I had paid for my flight to Las Vegas already and my hotel was booked, but I needed spending cash, so I didn't have complete control of it but after that I was good. I was going to Las Vegas a month after my son was born, at the time it was great her family was in town to help with the baby, so I was Scott free. Young minded not ready for a family me, thought like that, I now realized my wife needed her husband at home, but I can't change the past and Las Vegas was calling, The Cinco de Mayo fight between Pacquiao and Mosely was calling.

My first trip to Las Vegas didn't disappoint, we get off the plane then take a shuttle to our hotel, soon after we check in and go to explore the hotel we get approached by a group of women, there were six of them and the four of us, some of the women in the group were disinterested immediately, it was a game of musical chairs and two people were going to get left out, so of course, not to be mean but the ugly ones in the group start saying " girl lets go". It's always the ugly ones throwing a wrench in the plans. TJ was the main one interacting with them, me being newly and happily married, I stayed away but close enough distance to hear the conversation, the group made plans to meet up at the club later that night. Vegas was off to a great start. We meet that night, we had a fun time nothing too interesting, unfortunately this was their last night in town so there wasn't much else to that story. The next day being the rookies we were we wake up super early because of the excitement of being in Las Vegas. We went walking around exploring the strip like the tourist we were, we hit the wax museum, clowned around in there for a bit, next up we hit a fast food place, we pretty much lived off of fast food our whole time there we were all broke, especially me, it was cheap and easy and plus we were trying to get into the fight. We got there on a Monday anticipating meeting a few fighters, getting some autographs, but being the amateurs we were, we missed the fighter entrance, the fighter entrance is a formality that is a boxing promotion tradition, where the fighters make their walk through the lobby of the hotel hosting the fight, all the fight fans gather in an attempt to get an autograph or a picture, tired and trying to beat the heat we go back to our hotel room like novices, we turn on ESPN and wouldn't you know it, the fighters are right down the street making their entrance to the hotel's lobby. We rush down there but dammit we're too late, no Mosely, no Pacquiao. Surely we thought we would get another chance to meet them but nope, the closest we would get is meeting Manny Pacquiao's trainer Freddie Roach, super nice guy by the way, he took a picture with us, chatted with us for a second and signed the Pacquiao hat I had, we also got a chance later to meet Kelly Pavlik, the former middleweight champ who was fighting that Saturday and Antonio Tarver. I hated Antonio Tarver for beating Roy Jones Jr., but it was cool to meet fighters for the first time, so I got his autograph. That night we went to the club and we ran into another group of women not nearly as cute as four of the six that had first approached us, but they were fun. So, after the club we plan on moving on and doing our own thing for the rest of the night, but they had other plans. The girls invite us to their hotel room upstairs where we find two or three other women in the room who didn't feel like going to the club that night, they're like seven deep in one room. Have you ever been in a situation where you tell

103

someone bye multiple times, but they still don't get the hint they just keep talking and making plans, that's exactly where Marcus, TJ, ZO, and I found ourselves? In an attempt not to be rude we pretend to be interested as they kept making plans involving us. Apparently, they weren't buying the jet lag excuse, or they didn't care, so they volunteered to meet us downstairs in the lobby after they got dressed, we said ok. We decided to ditch them once we left the room, but they were women on a mission. These girls got undressed and dressed so fast, they had to set a woman's world record for getting dressed. We had been walking around the lobby of their hotel trying to find our way out, they found us before we could find an exit, so now we're walking through the lobby with them as they start flirting with us, we get a good look at them out of club clothes and makeup in good lighting...God please fix it. There's no need to be rude but they must not be too keen on social cues in Tennessee, which is where they were from. We tried to escape politely, but the only way out was for us to be assholes, it was Vegas in the middle of the week, nothing else to do, so why not entertain them. We decide to walk to Fat Burger, I guess as a conversational piece the loudest one of the group, who happened to be all over TJ, wanted to let him and everyone else know that she only spent three hundred and fifty dollars to get to Vegas, I guess she didn't appreciate our lack of enthusiasm because she repeated herself three or four times, " Three fifteh", "Three fifteh for air'thang" "Three fifteh for air'thang that's all we paid y'all". TJ was visibly annoyed. I remember thinking to myself, will this country fried heffer go sit her ass down somewhere, y'all piled up in that room like a damn clown car, three of y'all sleeping on the floor, three hundred fifty dollars to get to Las Vegas is reasonable. ZO meanwhile was hanging with the only cute one in the group so he was doing ok, so I thought, keep in mind cute is relative in this situation, ZO was trying to figure a way out too, the girl the whole walk he was with was nibbling on his neck feeling her way around testing the potentiality of a kiss. He responds with light petting as not to be mean, I could see his face every now and then as we walk down the Las Vegas strip and all I could say in my head "Is better you than me". I wanted to laugh so bad, but I didn't want to jinx myself or be rude, she finally says that she wants to kiss him before the night is over, loud enough for one of the girls to say "oop get em". ZO turned around as subtly as he could to signal for help, but we were all hemmed up. I tried not to be obvious and make eye contact with him so I kept looking straight, then I turned to pretend to look at something else, but I could feel him looking at me. I continue to walk with the woman that's with me and I babble on about my new wife and baby boy, I did that on purpose. You could almost see the air being sucked out of her night understanding it wasn't happening, she probably thought to herself damn he's married, why did I have to get the good guy. We make our way to Fat Burger, I think what finally did it for ZO was after the girls ordered their burgers the girl who attached herself to him, hopped up to fix her order and said "oooh hold on, I want extra uhh'nions". I could make this shit up, but I promise you I'm not. The horror and disgust on his face to this day makes me laugh. ZO escaped that night without having to kiss her, we all escaped that night after some haggling and explaining we would catch up with them tomorrow night, finally the jet lag excuse was working, luckily our hotel was too far for them to walk. We spent parts of the trip dodging them the rest of the time we were there, hoping to spot them before they saw us, but even then, that was fun. We were determined not to hang out with them again. Don't get me wrong they really were good people, in "Sin City" that's a big compliment, I truly hope they enjoyed the rest of their trip, but it wasn't happening with us. As the weekend gets closer the city gets packed, it was great, the fight itself fell on "Cinco de Mayo" so the city was really buzzing. We go to the weigh-in but we ultimately didn't see the fight in person, as ticket scalpers in the fight game are the scum of the earth, they hiked the ticket prices up too high for guys on a budget like us, so we sat in one of our rooms and streamed the fight. We went out that night after the fight, we had a good time nothing memorable, the next day was Sunday and the trip was over, time to go back to reality.

Returning from Vegas still on a high, I come home to my new in-laws still there, it was time for they ass to go home. I know they were there because I wasn't, and looking back on it, me in Vegas as a new husband and father wasn't a good look, so I could only imagine what was going through their heads, but............ it was time for they ass to go home. I wanted to enjoy my family and my new wife, I got it, thank you for all y'all help. I didn't say it, but I was thinking it. When your married you can't always think about yourself, but I was too immature to really understand the full grasp of that. She needed her family and she needed me; she needed all the support she could get. I wish I understood postpartum depression, but when it's happening, and you're young, sometimes you just think about yourself and how someone makes you feel. I was forgetting the golden rule "Happy wife, happy life".

To make thing worse on the way to my summer job at the local mental health facility. I was working there before grad school started to make ends meet. I get a text from Melissa the first and only woman I had ever been in love with. I do the right thing and keep it surface level, but, and there is a big but, I didn't update her what had been going on the past eleven months in my personal life. I was embarrassed for some reason in that moment, I didn't tell her I was married with a kid now, especially not with a woman I would meet out of town a month or so after we broke up, I wasn't up for explaining that timeline and I didn't want her to try to piece it together because sometimes our imagination is way worse than reality. Reality was it was so dumb, I was proud of my family but her text did something, it wasn't a reminder of what her and I used to be, that was always with me, but a reminder of the thought I had in the back of my head ever since my wedding day, I don't know what I'm doing and maybe this was a mistake. Text messages are great it gives you enough time to respond with the right words or a better lie than you would have had on the fly. Side note, to all the love birds out there, call your mate, hear their voice, let them tell you in a phone call, you won't get the full picture because you won't get facial expressions and body language, but it's way easier to lie through text than in real time on the phone. She would later find out I had a family now anyway, and we ceased communications for good. The jokes about women being detectives were real, I didn't know how she found out nor did I care as much as I would have if my son wasn't here, but it was better that way, my family needed my complete attention

My in laws left, we started arguing shortly after that, and the arguments got worse, I just didn't understand what she wanted, she didn't have to work, I got a summer job to get us through, I was working on a career, I was there for the baby, she was just tripping. The reality of postpartum depression eluded my dumbass. I wasn't there for her. The arguments got worse and that brand-new feeling wore off. Graduate school starts and my schedule really picks up, but relief comes in the form of loan money from school, I used it to help supplement her not working. It had been a hell of a year at that point, I graduated from undergrad, I started a graduate program, I had my first son, I got married, the money was a relief, even if it was loan money. Anything I could do outside of asking family for money worked for me. I was proud to take care of my family on my own, which is why when her car broke down, an incident occurred that would become a reoccurring point of contention in our marriage. We needed to get her a new car, we talked about not needing another bill so a brand-new car was out of the question, we really couldn't afford a car note. So I scoured the internet and I find it, the perfect car, nothing fancy but it's in our budget with the loan money I had left and it's just something to get from a to b so she can take the baby to the hospital or she could go to the store. I didn't want her stuck in the house no more than she wanted to be stuck there. So, we needed two cars, the hours I worked and being in graduate school just didn't work, it was too much to ask of her for her to be responsible for me. I pick the car up with TJ, at this point there's only three of us left in town Marcus is in bootcamp and ZO was going to be busy around that time. I can't lie I felt like I did it, I was driving back and TJ was following me driving my car and I just thought to myself I'm doing this family thing, son your dad is a problem solver, wife you get on my damn nerves but look at this I still handle business look at the man you got! I didn't get the reception I thought I would she wasn't impressed at all, see I tried to surprise her, she was surprised alright, but she wasn't happy with the car. Two months later comes the part where I get pissed, she goes behind my back and borrows money from her father, trades in the car I got her to get the car she "deserves" in her words. I was "mad than a Mufucka" excuse my language. I felt a small sense of betrayal, I thought we were in this together, I'm handling the bills. You couldn't have ran that by me? The strongest feeling I felt was that huge hit to my ego, you had to go to another man for help, I don't give a damn if it was your father. Did she not trust me to be the head of household? That shit was disrespectful, so we argued about that a lot and then I gave in, not because I was thinking happy wife happy life, but it was pointless the car was here. Now that I think about it, she could have figured I wasn't much help when she was going through postpartum depression, some head of household he was, when I needed him most, he argued with me instead of trying to understand me, if that's what my wife felt, fair point. I left her to figure it out. Well intended or not that's what I did. Weeks passed and I get a letter that got my mind off things, we all get a letter from Marcus, he wants to go back to Vegas when he gets out of training and gets settled at his duty station. He's saying he might be able to pull it off in May. Hell yes, I needed this.

As I'm working my way through grad school, my wife and I get into a routine, things are working, but to say we were both happy was a bit of a stretch, but in the grand scheme of things we were grateful, our son was healthy, and we were making ends meet. An opportunity came up for me. A professional conference for grad school was coming up and guess what, it was in Miami! So, after a little begging and persuading about how this could help me get a job in the future, she's ok with me going, but a man can't go hunting without his dogs, TJ and ZO volunteer their services. We had all wanted to see The Miami Heat's big three of Lebron James, Dwayne Wade, and Chris Bosh live, and wouldn't you know it, it was basketball season. So we go down to Miami, have a great time at the game, head to the strip club, it's Miami I had never been and being in Miami, in my mid-twenties, strip clubs are kind of the thing to do, especially if you're a tourist and one of the guys that's with you is a local and knows the best strip clubs in town. In my defense I did attend all the seminars in the daytime and left TJ and ZO to their own devices, but at night we had fun. Too much fun, ZO had reconnected with some girls he knew down there, one for me, one for TJ, just as a wingman there was nothing salacious going on, for some reason we all go to the strip club again. It's getting late and the next day we're supposed to leave, TJ utters out of nowhere, being all mature and shit and says, "Hey man we need to call it a night.". We blow him off. The fun guy is trying to be responsible? In hindsight he was on to something, the conference was over and it was time to call it a night, so of course we stay out until 9am the next morning and the sun is out, that's when we finally decided to head back to the hotel to get a cat nap, checkout and then hit the road. But nobody is in any condition to drive back to Tallahassee. So, I tell my wife and shockingly she was ok with it, probably because it's hard to argue with someone when you're by yourself, she was enjoying her time without me around to irritate her, we needed a break. So the guys and I hatch a plan to be responsible, we are going to check into another hotel, cheaper this time so we're saving money and sleep all night, then be ready to leave early in the morning before the sun catches us, but first it was too early, check in wasn't until three in the afternoon, so we decided to walk around the mall when it opens to kill time before our 3pm check in. We get to the hotel at around 1am the next day to check in. At this point we have failed miserably at being responsible, and we were working on one hour of sleep. A walk around the mall can be distracting, especially when those same girls we hung out with the night before were making plans with us. TJ once again told us after 3pm hit and we didn't check in our room like we planned, we need to stop playing and get to the room. The world was coming to an end. TJ said we need to stop playing. But when one of the girls we were with in a very ZO like moment asked " You somebody daddy?" he let it go and smiled like he knew we were messing up, but in reality it was just me that was messing up, that's who he was really speaking to. I was the married one. We got to the hotel and get checked in around 1am, but the night wasn't over. ZO invited the girls over to our room, I was complicit in it, it was fun living single for a minute. After a while ZO asked, "What's taking them so long?". "Hey bruh call em, my phone bout to die." I had one of the girl's number just in case we all got separated from earlier, which we did. So, I scroll down my call log and call. Ring, ring …...Hello? Me: Hey where y'all at? The room number is ###, just head up the stairs through the back when y'all get here. The response from the phone was, "What are you talking about?", it didn't register to me, so I said the name of the hotel, they were clearly confused. Then I hear, you know this me right, your wife? Oh shit! I called my wife. No sleep is a bitch. TJ is watching what's happening in real time, so after I scramble and tell my wife oh no, I thought I was talking to one of ZO's homeboys, "Baby, Yo' voice sounded deeper than a mug when you answered." He looks me in the eye, he knows exactly what just happened, he takes off out the door down the hallway to bust out laughing so my wife won't hear. He returns with ZO to diffuse the situation and vouch for me. She kind of bought it I think, I will never really know for sure, but nothing happened that night I was a faithful husband as I had always been, I wanted my family. After my wife and I hung up, the guys and I laughed about it, we had a few drinks, we let the girls know after we hang with them for a minute, we need to get some rest and they leave around 3am.

Upon return I get that "mmm hmm ZO's homeboy" comment half-jokingly for a while, but it wasn't a major event in our marriage. Plus a few months later Marcus would get a break from training and Vegas was around the corner, so I had to finesse my way back into her good graces. That next year, the finish line in grad school was approaching, it was going to be time to move again because for my last year I had to complete a one year internship, the problem was I needed to get paid while I was doing it, my wife was still not working. Just my luck the only place paying interns was the one place I didn't want to go back to, home. Vegas comes and goes it was fun, nothing to write home about other than seeing Marcus with barely any hair looking like a naked mole rat, it had been a minute. The year passes my son is a year older, I love watching him grow, I think my wife and I both got lost in him, but now it's time to get placed for my internship. I accept the internship back home as the money dictated. It was just ZO and TJ left in Tallahassee, they were working on their PHDs and in serious relationships, the team was basically broken up, Marcus got stationed in North Carolina and I was back home. We kept in contact through group text, talking about upcoming fights, discussing times we could all get together, which is how we settled on Las Vegas being our annual thing around fight week, specifically Cinco de Mayo.

Before we move back home, I get some shocking news, baby number two is on the way. Months later I would find out we're having a boy, man I can't miss, back to back boys I was feeling pretty good. It was kind of perfect timing, home wasn't so bad, my wife was able to finally start working, see being back home meant our families could help with our son and we didn't need daycare, her family wasn't too far away from my hometown, which meant more money in our pockets. Life was

116

good and I was returning to Vegas with way more money than the broke grad student who had been there the last few years, she was working and technically so was I. That February, my son is born and guess what, my internship will be over in a few months and I will graduate soon, then Las Vegas, sounds familiar? My son is born and I'm just as excited as the first time. I'm getting the hang of this marriage thing and I think I'm doing pretty good in fatherhood. My wife begins to understand that the guys trip to Vegas is mostly about boxing, I come back with autographs and souvenirs that my sons will have well after I'm gone, my wife and I are starting to see eye to eye. April comes and I graduate. They liked me so much at my internship they offer me a job. I don't get to stay in the department I interned in, but I get switched to a new department where they felt like they could use me best. It didn't bother me when I was notified, because it would be nice to get a new experience in a new place. The demographics of my new department were a little different, it was younger, and mostly female, no matter, I'm older and much more mature than when I first went to college surrounded by a sea of young women, plus nothing could compare to college and I have a family now. If

I could survive Miami and years of Las Vegas, dodging any workplace advances would be too easy.

I'm getting comfortable three months in; home is home now. It works because my wife doesn't have to switch hospitals in a new city, we don't even need to move a couch we're already set. Life is moving along pretty well, my wife seemed happy my second baby boy was healthy, the couple that started off rocky weathered the storm.

Things were moving along so well that wouldn't you know it, seven months later she's pregnant again. I mean not to brag but, that's what I do! I'm too strong! three strong! I'm the Oprah of this baby making business, you get a baby! You get a baby! Ya mammy can get a baby, just let me know! At least that's what I'm thinking until she tells me, "I'm not having this baby!". It wasn't even a real discussion she just told me straight up. I'm all for women's choice, but this was different, I was being dictated to and we were a family. She had to give birth; I get it. I'm not caring the baby, I get it. It's not going to alter my body and I wasn't the perfect caretaker with our first son, but I was better now, but apparently not enough. We have discussions about it on and off for a couple of weeks. She was steadfast in our discussions, well I'm being nice they were arguments but not crazy loud arguments, our kids were home. I understood her points, but it was so flimsy, we had family there to help us, it just boiled down to she didn't want it, her exact words were "I just don't want to have it". It felt like a rejection, rejection of me as a man, a father and a husband. I know that was a selfish perspective, but it was clear the idea of our family and how it was going greatly differed like night and day. We cool off for a couple of days I come home, and she is in the bed, she says she doesn't feel well so I leave her alone about the baby, after a few days she's feeling better, she invited me out to dinner after work. She already sent the kids to her father's, so the weekend was ours. I know what it's about and I'm hoping she changed her mind. The car ride over is stale, we are pleasant to each other but there is clearly something hovering over our heads, but the car ride is not the time, she had intended to have this conversation once we got settled at our table. We get to the restaurant, we get seated, there was tension in the air, nerves, pressure, all of it, I mean it felt like a first date. I began going through the possible scenarios in my head maybe she is here to convince me in a civil way she's not having the baby and she's buttering me up with a steak dinner or maybe she had a change of heart. The last thing I was thinking was what came next. She tells me she had the abortion. There's a long pause, fuck this restaurant I'm about to turn this bitch out I'm thinking. We try that whisper arguing but we're still attracting attention. I get especially loud when she tells me how it happened. We had joint accounts so where did you get the money from? There wasn't anything unusual coming out of the account. I would always check even though we were doing a lot better financially. I had just been accustomed to watching our pennies, so I would know if there was a crazy charge on there, apparently, she did too, which is why she went to her father for the money. Her bitch ass father, I still want to lay hands on this man to this day. Was I not a man to him? That's just bad business interjecting yourself in another man's marriage like that, you liable to get yo' ass whooped, which is exactly what I wanted to do. I know he was supporting his daughter, but damn you cut me off at the knees, you buy her a new car and then you help in aborting our baby your future grandchild. Her stepmother was ok with this? What kind of family is this? That's some sorry shit, I didn't like my in-laws anyway, what man does, but I hated they ass now for this. Then I began thinking, our family isn't that bad, what if she had other reasons, like she didn't know for sure if the baby was mine. Once that thought entered my mind, for some reason that seemed to make more sense to me than anything. The same family that was happy for a shotgun wedding, probably would do whatever they could do to protect their daughter from the consequences of an adulterous affair that would lead to a child out of wedlock.

We leave the restaurant, so we can have the real showdown at home. The car ride is mixed with yelling, telling me to watch the road, me talking shit about her family and her defending them. I will admit when you're as angry as I was things come out of your mouth that may be true, but you shouldn't say under any circumstances, like her hoe ass sister that had like four kids with three or four different guys. I hated their family gatherings, I had to help with all them bad ass kids. I ended up questioning her faithfulness. We argue about that all the way into the house. I will always wonder about it, but I will never really know the truth, but if she did cheat on me, she deserves an Oscar. For a time she was calm throughout the argument, she expected what was coming from me, but when I questioned her fidelity, I guess to her it came out of left field or I touched a nerve, either way that's when either she put on an Oscar worthy performance and she was lying or I was wrong. I would never really know what happened and that ate at me more than the fact that her father helped her. I had to take her word for it, but how could I when she had gone behind my back and made decisions without me, big decisions that affected our family. Things were never really the same after that, we had a family that was in front of our face to take care of, but we weren't companions, we were just parents. As time passes we both get lost in work and our family, things smooth over I guess, but family gatherings are awkward to say the least, her father attempted to talk to me every time we came around , but he rarely touches the real point of contention with me. I lost a lot of respect for him, I saw myself at times in mid conversation slapping the shit out of him, but we all can't get what we want, unless you're my wife. We have a few laughs with the kids around every now and then, but we argue much more now. I hope she was happy; I mean she was doing what she wanted to do without my input, who wouldn't be happy? Can't forget the golden rule, happy wife, happy life, right? We held it together and kept doing the three things we became good at; arguing, tending to our kids and "physical activity." on occasion. It felt like we weren't a couple anymore, we both felt it, but it was easier to focus on our kids. Damn I needed a Vegas trip with my guys.

Chapter V

Vegas Veterans

April is here! It's not Cinco De Mayo but Manny is fighting so we made an exception. We weren't high rollers in Las Vegas but that didn't mean we couldn't make the most of it, in our minds we were becoming regulars, this year Pacquiao was fighting a rematch with Timothy Bradley. The highlights on this trip I will never forget for a lot of reasons, it was a turning point for me and just a hell of an experience. We were at the weigh-in before the fight and after it was over, we saw Roy Jones Jr., Max Kellerman, and Jim Lampley still lingering around, probably doing work for HBO. Roy Jones Jr. unanimously being one of our favorite boxers, Max and Jim however were commentators, but they were boxing mainstays, if you watched a big fight chances are you saw their faces or heard their voice, so if you could get a picture with one of them, you took the opportunity. After the arena starts to clear we see the lucky select few on the lower levels, wondering aloud how they got access to the back, we watch them stream to the back of the stage where the fighters would be, so we got the idea to stick around and maybe we'll meet a few people. We could still see Roy and the guys from where we were in the stands after everyone started clearing out, so instead of waiting we decided to walk around this maze of an arena in an attempt to meet Roy, at this point we had tried several times , but we were never successful. So, we ran behind the stands thinking we had access to them, we ran so far to the point we arrive at these set of double doors, we hoped they were leading to where Roy was. We figure the door is locked, nobody would be crazy enough to leave them open, so we were just going to wait there, but what the hell, why not give it a try. I turn the handle expecting some sort of resistance, but it turns, I pull, and it opens, we all say, "oh shit". The last thing we thought was that door was going to be unlocked. We make our way through the hallway marveling at all the posters of the legendary fighters on the wall, we walk past a few dressing rooms and we look up and see Manny Pacquiao's lifelong friend Buboy Fernandez with his family, we stop to take a picture, then to the right we see more people, we walk through and we hear "Hey!". We thought we were caught; I know in my head I thought damn party over. "I like your shoes". It had to be someone from Manny's camp, he was decked out in his gear, he stopped us to compliment Marcus on his shoes, he had one of the older editions of Pacquiao's shoes on. We keep walking to where we hear the most commotion and we look up and realize we are walking through the fighters entrance, this is the very same path they take to enter the ring, just then TJ starts bouncing up and down like a fighter making his way to the ring, he's such a big ass kid, we're all excited but we try to blend in like we're supposed to be there. We walk through and we start seeing media of all sorts then we see Evander Holyfield, we don't ask for an autograph because he's talking to someone and the last thing we needed was someone to notice and ask for credentials, so we just keep wondering around this sea of people. While we are wandering around getting a glimpse of all the people and faces we recognize we see an even more familiar face cross our line of sight, Freddie Roach Manny's trainer, I remember how nice he was the first time we met him so I figured I would ask him for a picture and an autograph because he had yet to attract the attention that the other stars in the area had. I had training mitts this time not a hat from one of his fighters, he happily signs and we take pictures, we jokingly ask him about the fight and he entertains us with an answer, we thank him and walk away as to not wear out our welcome or for someone to start asking questions. We walk and just then ZO says hey the fighters are right there being interviewed. ZO to this point was silent, this probably meant the most to him out of all of us because this was literally part of his childhood. While we played videogames and did what kids our age would have been doing on most Saturday nights, he would tell me stories about when he was little, staying up on a Saturday night to watch fights. We make our way over to the fighter interviews with the biggest smile on our face trying to fit in, but if anyone took a closer look, they would see we had our phones out recording to capture the moment, not for work but just as star struck fans. After we leave in and effort not to press our luck, and people were starting to clear out, we were still disappointed we didn't get a chance to meet Roy, but we had a great experience.

We're officially Las Vegas veterans, Las Vegas wasn't new to us anymore, we had come a long way from the rookies who were snapping pictures on the strip every two seconds to seasoned veterans that walked past iconic Las Vegas staples without much pause. We finally had a look behind the curtain most fans won't get. It was Marcus that pointed out that we were used to Vegas as we strolled down the strip in between us bragging about what just happened, "Man we don't even take pictures like that anymore", and it was true. We only took pictures at this point with fighters we haven't yet met, and that list was getting shorter by the year, especially after what we experienced that whole week, it was truly a once in a lifetime experience. Las Vegas was our refuge now, our playground with our usual spots, not some exciting new city we had unrealistic expectations of. We weren't in awe of the bright lights anymore, now don't get me wrong the lights were great, Las Vegas wouldn't be Las Vegas without them, but they were supposed to be there, and so were we. Vegas was now our stomping ground, gone was the Caf, gone was the local boxing club, Las Vegas became the place where we met up, but it wasn't madden debates or boxing discussions anymore, we were there and the talks of who was going to win the fight was mute because it was coming in a matter of days. It was to catch up on life, to talk about our new experiences and to make some, we talked about our kids, well Marcus and I discussed our kids. Marcus and Leah recently had their first son. You could see the newness and the happiness on his face, I remember that feeling too well. Marcus would also have a big announcement before this most recent trip, he and Leah were finally getting married. They had been together for years, ever since freshman year so we were wondering when it was coming. This Las Vegas trip had a new wrinkle, it was essentially a bachelor party for Marcus, what a great experience for him considering all that had just happened at the weigh in, I never had a bachelor party, so I was happy for him. We went on a party bus which was different but other than that we stuck to the normal routine of boxing related activities. Another highlight for me personally was his proposal, not just because I was happy for my boy, but the effect it had on me. We finally ask him once we get a moment of downtime in the room how he did it. The details of his proposal were in stark contrast to my fly by night proposal. I listen as Marcus detailed it: *So bruh she had been bringing up marriage but I was getting* adjusted to military life and I just wasn't ready for that married life, I can't lie bruh I was fresh out of training, I got to my duty station, and there were some bad ass female officers bruh, I wanted to dip off into something right quick, but you know I wasn't going to do Leah like that, she had been holding it down, so I did right, I wasn't going nowhere anyway, we done been through it, I wasn't about to start over, you know what I mean trade in old problems for some new ones . So later she gets pregnant and you already know she turned up the pressure on ya boy. So, man, I play that shit just right until my little man born. I convince her we should focus on her having a healthy pregnancy because you know how stress can affect women 'round that time, but about seven months in, I had already made up my mind I was gonna ask her to marry me at some point. I was just gonna wait until after the baby. So, my baby boy gets here and I'm home with her for about two weeks, but it worked out because Christmas was about a month and a half away, so I get that time off too. She finally get out the house and we leave the baby with her people, they had came up for Christmas. We hit the mall and we walk pass the jewelry story. I was waiting for it bruh I knew she was gonna say something about a wedding ring, I complain, so now she thinks she convinced me

*to go in, she says "Oh I just want to look for fun.",
fun my ass bruh, I let her run her mouth though, we
were going in anyway. I know her, she was really
going to be on that marriage tip after the baby, so we
go in there and I tell her to pick out any ring she
wants because it's just for fun. She picks out one of
the most expensive rings and I fake like I'm mad
because of the price, the chick working the counter
tries to convince me, but I say hell nah hahaha. Leah
embarrassed as shit, she mad boy, she turn around
and leave, when she turn around, I signal to ole girl
I'll be back. Leah goes to the bathroom before we leave
the mall and I rush back and setup an appointment
with the sales lady. Later that week I go back to get
the ring. I'm proposing on the upcoming Valentine's
day, I figured she would love that shit you know how
women are, I planned it out, she had been bothering
me about a horse and carriage ride through the city
for a minute, to be real I did not want to sit in the
back of a cart smelling a horses ass for thirty minutes,
but I figured I owed her. I call the place and they have
a marriage proposal package. The night I'm
proposing we go to dinner first, so after dinner right
before the bill comes, I act like I have to use the
bathroom, I had to make sure that the lady was
outside by the horse buggy with a sign that says*
"Free horse and carriage rides, I work for tips".

Once we leave the restaurant, I make sure we walk by so she can see the lady because I know she's gonna ask to get on, so I finally act like I give in, and she's happy as shit bruh.

We riding through the city, I can't lie man it's straight, we riding for a minute then she takes us to a secluded park and pretends the horse has a hurt hoof , horseshoe or whatever horses got and tells us we can go take a walk...... As Marcus goes on telling the story I think like damn he must really love her, they want to be together. It wasn't a comparison I was making, well not on purpose at least, it was just a random thought because I never thought about going through that much trouble to make anything that special for my wife, but not out of any disdain or lack of caring, I cared about my wife. Our life had just been moving so fast, I had never given it much thought during this whole time. Do we really want to be together? How can I make her day special? I was her husband and the father of her kids it was implied in the title she was special, right? We were supposed to be together we had a family; this wasn't all for nothing.

I arrive back home after this latest Vegas trip, I let my wife know before my plane takes off, she doesn't need to have the kids out this late to pick me up from the airport, my cousin could come to pick me up. When I arrive home, I walk up to the front door and it's a different feeling, I was now wondering about a lot, like how my wife truly felt about me, not whether I was a competent caretaker anymore but was I the man she wanted. I came through the door, my boys are walking and talking now so they race towards the door, my oldest wins, it's easy to get distracted by them as I come through the door. I hear "Dad!" as I'm greeted with hugs. I show my boys some of the things I have for them, I let them play with the gloves that I didn't get autographed, as my wife walks up to greet me with a kiss, she pauses before she gets to me for a second to watch my boys and I interact, I can see her out of the corner of my eye smiling. We kiss, she ask me how the fight was, my time with the guys, then she makes a halfhearted joke about me being on good behavior, "You better not had been flirting with any women or I'm a cut it off!" we both laugh and just like that, my questions of our relationship slowly dissipate. I'm not worried about the thoughts of our marriage, it was still a question in the back of my mind, but this wasn't the time for that, we were all happy I was home. I was her husband, I'm home with my family and that's all that mattered.

It doesn't take much time for us to get back into our normal routine, her busy with work and the boys and me getting lost in work again. Work was work nothing special the new department was now just my department and when you spend enough time around any group of people every day, you become social. I was one of three guys in my department, so we naturally gravitated towards each other, well not so much with one of the guys as he was the head of the department, but we still had our guy talk, sports, upcoming events etc. My department was young and female but completely professional, at first. I began to get a different view of the department when my coworker, let's call him John, John tells me he's sleeping with one of the girls in the department and she's married, I find it hard to believe until he shows me the text messages and pictures. I personally don't believe in doing that, but I'm not going to tell another grown man how to handle his business, having sex with a married woman is bad enough, but telling people, that's bad business, we weren't even boys like that for me to know that or at least that was my perspective as he was telling me the story. I found it even harder to believe before he showed me the text messages because the married woman he was sleeping with was also pregnant and she was showing. To be honest I had never heard of that, I had always heard of shitty men cheating on their pregnant wives, but this was a first for me. Over time I would get past the facade of professionalism and work would become a little too social. I had one woman make an advance subtly, she started with questions, how long was I married, how many kids I had, what did my wife do, then after a few weeks of probing she finally asked me out for drinks with the group, It was subtle, but I could tell what was going on, which prompted me to put a picture of my wife and kids on my desk to diffuse all potential questions or advances, and it worked, at least for the first woman that approached me. I figured it would've worked as a blanketed statement for any woman thinking about approaching me, the pictures was my way of saying "Hey I'm happily taken", without having to even have the conversation, but when a woman's determined to get what she wants, she takes it as a challenge, not a keep away sign. The next time I was approached at work, it would be a different woman with a very different approach, I don't know whether she thought her coworker wasn't my type or she just thought she was that much better than her. She walks into my office sees my picture of my wife and kids, and without hesitation presses me on what my wife and I do for fun and if I wanted to grab dinner with her one day after work because I seemed "interesting", whatever the hell that means. See I began to understand the questions about my wife. It was just those women sizing up the competition, none of them who approached me were generally interested in my wife, it was just a breast measuring contest.

When declining advances of any woman you must be careful, too harsh and you've made an enemy, too nice and you give the impression there's interest and it's only a matter of time before you give in. I can only imagine how difficult it is for a woman in the same predicament, when a man shows interest in her and she's not able to respond the way she'd like. As for me, in that moment I tell her I'm busy and it probably wouldn't work because my wife wouldn't go for that. At this point I wanted to talk to John about it, but he was sleeping with a pregnant married woman he wouldn't understand my predicament nor care, so I confided in Nicki. Nicki was my coworker, but she was on the up and up, she never approached me about anything that wasn't professional, and any friendly conversations we had were about sports, our college years, or our kids. Nicki and I had formed a bond we didn't need to exchange numbers because everyone in the department had everyone's contact information for professional reasons anyway, it was a way to have an open line of communication for sudden meeting changes and updates. When Nicki and I would communicate through text, it wasn't anything to be suspicious of, it was always just friendly conversation.

Nicki had become my buddy, not in a romantic interest type of way, but I could trust her, I felt comfortable telling her things. I could tell her the things I couldn't tell my wife, or I didn't want to tell my boys. I talked about my frustration with a few women at work and how messy they were with their attempts to enter my marriage. She felt my pain, she agreed that those women were dirty, especially because they were pursuing a man that was trying to do the right thing. I could tell her anything. I could tell Nicki the things I was too prideful to tell my boys about like my wife's abortion, or everything I had experienced; my in-laws, the arguments I had with Tarah, and my displeasure with her attitude towards me as a caretaker and provider. Nicki was there to listen, she was my psychologist, I could tell her things, and she would just listen to me and not judge. She respected me and my opinion. She even had words of wisdom and insight on some of the problems I had experienced, see she had been married so she understood the struggle of married life. She experienced hurt in her marriage, her husband cheated on her, she felt like she did everything right, but it wasn't enough, she didn't feel like she was enough, especially after she took him back the first time and he did it again. We kept texting, after a while it was more personal than professional, but it was nothing out of the ordinary, just hey how's your day, did you catch the game, typical stuff, it was almost like I was talking with one of my boys. Work became an escape from home because she was there, whatever was going on at home, I had someone to vent to, whatever I was uncomfortable telling my wife or whatever I knew my wife wasn't going to be receptive to, she would be there to listen and with an open mind as well. She respected me, Niki would always tell me how good of a father I was, and I really appreciated that. She made my life easier. The annoying shit my wife said didn't irritate me as much anymore, life was good. Nicki even thought it was great that my boys and I started this tradition of going to Las Vegas. She said, "guys needed their guy time", my wife on the other hand was lukewarm on the issue, she let me go but it was grudgingly. I had it figured out, I had my friend at work who I could confide in, I had my boys and I had my family, life was great. Then it got even better, Floyd Mayweather and Manny Pacquaio had finally agreed to fight. This fight was it. This was the source of our most heated debates, what fighter was running from who, who would win and how, after ten years every barber shop argument, every fight party argument we ever had would finally be settled. It was so exciting, and you know we had to be in the city for this one. As we prepare for the fight for months, Nicki finds my enthusiasm amusing, while my wife's face every time I'm on the phone discussing plans with my boys has a permanent scowl.

Days before the fight my boys and I finalize plans for Las Vegas, ESPN has live shows being filmed, and we were going to attend. We're ready for the fight of the century, by this time Nicki and I had been texting and talking all the time at work and after work. Nicki and I had been getting close over the next several months, again nothing romantic but we just had a mutual appreciation for one another. We began talking even more than my wife and I did. She was so excited for me. Nicki knew how much I wanted to just be in the city even if we couldn't get into the fight. My wife takes me to the airport, I wait with her and my sons until it's time for me to go through my gate checks. We say a prayer, we kiss, and I hug my boys, tell them I love them, and then I'm off to the fight of the century. While waiting in the airport Nicki texts me and ask me if I boarded the plan yet and I tell her nope just waiting to get called. She replies and says she is going to miss me while I'm gone, "work won't be the same without you." She was being a bit dramatic I was only going to be gone a week. I jokingly reply you will get over it, John is there, and you have your other coworkers to keep you company. She sends me an eye roll emoji and says well whatever I'm going to miss you anyway. I don't know whether it was me being nice or it was what I really felt at the time, but I replied, "Ok, ok, u win I'm gonna miss u too". I didn't know I was going to miss her or not, hell I didn't think I was going to miss anybody I was going to have the time of my life. We get to Las Vegas and have a great experience all the sports talk shows we watch are on site doing meet and greets and live broadcasts, we finally meet Max Kellerman the commentator that was with Roy Jones Jr. the other year. We meet Stephen A. Smith and a few other ESPN sports personalities, anybody who's anybody is in Las Vegas and it seems like we got the chance to see or meet most of them.

TJ fresh out of a relationship, was so thirsty, to his credit one famous chick did give him the eye on our way to one of the events and he wouldn't shut up about it. To this day he talks about that shit. We're walking by the MGM food court going to the press conferences, well we are going to wait outside of the press conference hopefully to catch a few more boxers or boxing personalities, we had split up with ZO and Marcus, they went to see if they could catch up with another boxer to get his autograph. TJ and I are walking and we walk pass and older woman that gives him a slight pause and subtly looked him up and down behind her shades, I asked him who that was because she had on a press pass, I assumed she was a reporter and she might be able to get us in, highly unlikely but hey it's Vegas why not gamble for free. TJ responds with this big grin on his face, "You don't know who that was bruh? That's the ......momma!" He was right. The woman who checked him out was a very famous mother, who had daughters that were just as if not more famous than she was. She had recently and very publicly finalized her divorce under circumstances that were all over the cover of every magazine about two months prior. I say oh shit that's what's up, leave it up to this asshole to go on and on about it. He starts saying I could be her part time playboy blah blah blah, "Man why not, aye dog what you think? I should go back and say what's up huh?" I tell him go ahead because I know his scary ass wasn't about to do a damn thing, he's nervous talking to the waitress if she's pretty, there was no way in hell he had that kind of nerve so I knew he was bluffing, I just play along hoping he would shut up. As I'm trying to ignore him we run into an up and coming boxer, nobody really knows him yet so no crowds are following him, to tell you the truth I didn't know him either but TJ remembers the guy from the Olympics and says he's going to be a great one, so we stop and take pictures and have a conversation with a fighter named Errol Spence. TJ was goofier than usual this trip, I guess it was the setting, we were all buzzing more than usual, Las Vegas was alive, it was fight week and the fight of the century was on.

TJ and I stayed in the same room together so we would split up with Marcus and ZO every now and then to go get ready or just to get some down time from the strip. We split up one night to go back to our rooms to get some rest, Marcus and ZO go try to find a table to gamble at. TJ and I head to the room so we can rest up before going out again that night, just as we stop by our hotel bar to watch the last few seconds of an NBA playoff game, TJ gains the attention of a girl sitting at the bar, she has a friend with her so he tells me to come over with him "She was looking at ya boy". He's so damn scary but I get it, a man can't go hunting without his dawgs. So, we make our way over to the bar with TJ leading the way, I'm not much interested in her friend, but TJ is attempting to run some game with the one girl that smiled at him. After a while TJ is making progress, not that he isn't capable, but usually he is not the type to pick up some random woman. I guess his recent breakup had him in a different mood this trip, picking up random chicks was ZO's role in the group, to tell the truth that was my role too, but I had been out the game ever since my early days in college. We were just headed to the room to get some rest, but the game caught our attention, and then TJ caught someone's attention at the bar that altered his night. After I basically ignored the other girl, she lost interest, I wasn't the best wingman. She was ok looking, but I just wasn't up for entertaining her, I was tired we had all been up since four in the morning to get in line to be on a sports show that was broadcasting live. I let TJ know I'm going up to the room to get some rest, he looked like he had it from there. Almost two hours pass, and we start getting ready to head out for the night. I text TJ to see where he was, he lets me know he's on his way up. I tell him to hurry up we're all getting ready and don't make us late like he usually does. A few minutes later

144

while I'm ironing my clothes, I hear a knock on the door and I'm like who the hell is this knocking, it better not be TJ, this man has a key. Just as I walked to the door, I can hear the electronic key card activating the door to open. It's TJ, just as I get ready to ask him why the hell he didn't use his key I see the girl from the bar, I can tell he wasn't going out that night. I was happy for him, I talk to him for a bit and whispered jokingly when the girl goes to the bathroom, "Ok I see you bruh, just keep that shit away from my bed." We laugh quietly so she can't hear us. I start getting dressed, I speak to her out of courtesy and I'm out for the night. Little did I know I would be seeing her face more than I wanted to. The three of us are heading out and ZO asks where's TJ assuming he was late, ZO was ready to start talking shit, but I let him know, he's on a "solo mission". We all laugh, we're a little shocked to be honest TJ is the last guy we thought would deal with some random from a bar, but we were happy for him getting his "Las Vegas experience". After being out all night, I return to the hotel and head to the room, the TV is on, from the light I can see TJ and the girl still in his bed. I think to myself, what the fuck? Why is she still here? I didn't say anything I just get into my bed and go to sleep; it was a rare occasion; we beat the sun back to the hotel.

I wake up and she's still there, she's says good morning like she's supposed to be here, I say what's up real standoffish. I'm confused and slightly annoyed at this point, I'm thinking to myself, don't you have somewhere to be, and where the fuck is TJ. He comes out of the bathroom with a smile on his face once he knows I'm up, he says, "What up bruh?" I don't smile at all, he knows her ass needs to go, but she doesn't leave, even when we leave to go get something to eat, her ass is still laying comfortably in the bed. I asked him what the hell is she doing once we step outside the room to get something to eat because it was apparent, she has no plans of getting out of the bed. He explains, "Oh man she a local, her ac is out at her house, she's just staying for a little bit. She ain't hurting nobody, we can just leave her in the room, it's not like we're gonna be in there most of the day." Motherfucka what !? Are you serious? He's dead ass serious and I'm in disbelief, I'm not cool with leaving some random ass woman in the room with all my shit in there, this man is tripping. Also, it's a matter

146

of principal, she ain't pay for this Air Conditioning. He tries to convince me she's trustworthy, but I'm confused on how he knows that after one night, I had known this man for years and he's pulling this shit. I didn't trust anything anymore. We meet up with ZO and Marcus and they're ready to hear it all, TJ pulled some random chick from the bar, this only happens in Vegas, well only in Vegas for TJ, with his scary ass, ZO says "We have to hear this shit". Meanwhile I'm mad than a motherfucker. Come to find out, this girl is a porn actress, I had been so preoccupied with figuring out why she was still in our room, I didn't give much thought to where she came from, I just needed her to go back. I can't lie the fact that she did porn was cool; my boy pulled a porn actress. After the shock, we question this man like an FBI interrogation, we want to know everything after all she was in porn, so it wasn't like she was that private about her sex life. After we finish eating we get ready to go back to our rooms, we're still going on about it, but I ain't trying to stare this woman in the face as I try to relax in my room, so I say, we're heading to y'all room, it's cool because they want to hear more anyway. We get to the room and TJ finally shows us some of her work, he pulls up a few scenes she performed in on his phone, this girl was doing pregnant porn! We fall out laughing so hard, by this time I'm not as mad at TJ anymore but she still has to go. She had done some regular scenes he showed us but the first few scenes were pregnant porn, that shit was crazy. TJ tells us to "turn that shit off" he's getting defensive as we keep watching. ZO never missing a moment to talk shit, ZO starts messing with TJ, "Oh my bad bruh we ain't mean to make fun of yo' girl hahahaha, when y'all getting married bruh?" "Y'all can let the baby be the ringbearer, hahaha, that shit will be real cute". We start laughing even harder, TJ says man she had it rough, before he can say anything else ZO says, "I know, we see it Mufucka, she had it real rough!". At this point there's no reasoning, we are laughing too hard for TJ to get our attention. TJ was referring to the story she told him about needing money so that's why she did the scenes while she was pregnant, but we were only sympathetic to her child imagining growing up with that image of his or her mother. Porn actors and actresses, do it for the money so it wasn't a shock she participated in her profession for money. I specifically refer to her as an actress and not a star for a reason, we didn't know this woman from a can of paint, which is why I wanted her out, she could have been a great person, she did seem really nice, but I didn't want to take the chance to find out she wasn't as nice as she seemed. Having sex with a porn actress is a dope Vegas story though I will give him that. After another day of our resident porn actress enjoying our free AC, she finds another sucker or maybe she got the very strong vibe she wasn't welcomed. Either way after two days I was glad she was gone, communal bathrooms with a porn actress was too much Vegas for me. In between all the festivities and running around I text my wife every morning, but as frustrated as I was with TJ, I leave that story out, I talk to my sons before I start my day on the strip, I do miss them.

My wife and I talk but it's not for long. On the other hand, I'm texting Nicki any chance I get, she's way more interested in what I'm doing, she loves sports unlike my wife so when I reference some of the stars we met she understands my excitement. She tells me she misses me so I'm nice and say it back, I really don't miss anyone but my sons, but it is nice talking to her, she updates me about work just for conversation. She never calls I think she understands even though our relationship is platonic, we'd rather keep it a secret. Nobody would understand, especially my wife, and don't let anyone in our office get to talking, that would be a nightmare. See my life was different than everyone else's, Marcus and Leah were married with a kid, but they hadn't been through what my wife and I had. I bared the war wounds of a young married couple, now older who had to figure things out, and through the battles some things just lingered in our marriage like a bad odor and sour the relationship, so I did what I had to do to keep my family and my sanity. Marcus wouldn't understand, Leah and Marcus had a different relationship. Their relationship had been built purely from companionship not outside pressure, so it was a shock to me the night before the fight he says "Aye y'all I been wanting to try one of them massage parlors to see what they really bout, y'all tryna slide?" We look at him like shit why not we're just really piled up in the room chilling. While we're chilling, TJ's over here texting up a storm with the "preggo pornstar". We ride around town and find a massage parlor that looks like it may give more than a massage and Marcus says, "Shit that look like the one right there" so we pull in and park. He doesn't want to go in by himself and we weren't going to let him go alone anyway, we walk in and nobody's there. We ring the little concierge bell and wait, after a few minutes we began to leave but just as I touch the door I hear "Helloooo, Hi guys". I turned around and it's a *King Magazine* model, I don't even know if they were still making *King Magazine* back then but if they didn't they would bring back a special edition issue just for her, she was bad, not just pretty but the type of bad Uncle Luke raps about, she was thick, small waist everything. Excuse me "air'thang". Marcus still hanging around the desk starts smiling and says "Heeeeeeeeeey how you doing?" like he's about to try to get her number, he's a fool. They start chatting, I walk out and tell TJ and ZO to come in right quick they have to see her. By the time we trickle back in Marcus and the "Massage therapist" began discussing what he was looking for, that's when we leave them to it and head back to the car. We wait in the car cracking jokes about Marcus, they're cracking on me too calling us old married men,

TJ's talking shit until I remind him of his "pregnant porno wife". I didn't care what Marcus was doing as long as he was safe, but I was a little disappointed, I remember just six months ago being in Marcus's wedding standing there as a groomsman, like that's how you're supposed to do it, that's my "dawg". I was so happy for Marcus and Leah in that moment, but during our trip, if I had taken Marcus seriously, I would have seen this coming or at least heard his cries for help. I say that sarcastically but there's more truth to it being a cry for help than Marcus would ever admit. He was going around flirting with every group of women he saw on the strip, but that was just Marcus nothing unusual, he was just having fun, except in between his down time of pretending like he's Las Vegas's number one gigolo, he would mention, "Man you can get bored with the same woman." "We have over a decade in bruh" he said it a few times. I guess he had a moment of regret, Marcus was curious, I mean he did mention he saw a few Air Force women that piqued his interests before they got married, I guess being in the massage parlor was the manifestation of that. The certainty of marriage had gotten to him, this wasn't our first time to Las Vegas, he had never pulled this before, they hadn't even been married a full year yet, he had been faithful all this time but I guess it's just something about the words "I do" that changes everything. We waited for about ten to fifteen minutes then we see the door swing open, Marcus skips out like a kid or like TJ would, with a huge grin on his face. He opens the car door and hops in the back, we all started laughing, so we ask what happened minute man. "I couldn't do it bruh". In unison, the three of us say "Ahhhh this man"

Marcus: *All I could think about was Leah man, but not even just Leah bruh I was thinking about my damn son, that shit threw the whole vibe off.*

"Damn, my man conscious got the better of em'" ZO says, but not in normal ZO fashion, he wasn't talking shit this time, he follows up and says "that's good though bruh that shit wasn't worth it, especially if she was taxing, how much was she talking?"

Marcus: *Four hunnid bruh!*

Me: Damn!

TJ: **Damn!**

ZO: *Oh, hell nah! You did right B.*

ZO wasn't going to say man it's great you're being a good husband, and a great father, good job, we considered saying shit like that soft, so we just didn't talk like that, but we all knew what he meant. Marcus had come out those massage parlor doors like it was mission complete, like he had just fulfilled his long-time fantasy and he was finally satisfied. Marcus won't say this, but I think he came out with a smile, feeling happier than he's ever been, because in the moment when he backed out of his "massage" I think he realized how truly happy he was. He walked out with the knowledge of knowing that everything he needed and wanted was waiting for him at home, but this wasn't a soap opera so you wouldn't catch one of us in our weakest moment uttering some shit like that, well maybe TJ, who knows from the looks of it he was prepared to be stepdaddy with a Vegas one night stand. I'm being facetious of course.

Those rare occasions when wisdom is acquired without the usual accompanying of pain that a mistake inflicts, is life having mercy on us every once and awhile. It's not often we learn a valuable lesson in life and save four hundred dollars doing it. Having that sense of security and fulfillment must be nice. It was something I secretly wish I had, I did in a way, it just wasn't all at home, I had my family, a wife at my side, the security of true friendship and a listening ear at work.

Fight night comes and we have no luck, we find a few loose tickets but it's not worth sitting apart for fifteen hundred dollars in the nosebleed seats. Nicki was helpful in the process while we're running around looking for tickets. She did what she could by looking up ticket availability on the internet, it was pointless as I assumed, but it was nice of her to try. We end up at a local bar for a hundred bucks per person just to sit down and watch the fight, the night goes well for two of us. Mayweather ends up winning the fight by unanimous decision which leaves ZO and I pissed off, but TJ and Marcus vindicated. We were all Pacquiao fans, but TJ and Marcus drew the line at Mayweather. So, as they enjoy winning our 10-year argument we've been having, ZO and I sulk back to the car with disappointment. The trip felt like a bust, but that was just a knee jerk reaction to the night's events. So as we pack up the next day and get ready to head back to reality we do what we always do before we leave Las Vegas, talk about how much we don't want to leave, how much fun we had, the next potential big fight on the horizon and start planning the next year's trip. TJ and ZO leave the hotel together, they're heading back to Tallahassee. I'm going back home, and Marcus is going to California where he's now stationed. Man, I remember the first time we went to Las Vegas we left and came back together on the same flight, it was a minor detail but when we started going our separate ways after our trips, I realized what made Las Vegas wasn't Las Vegas but about us being together.

I'm traveling through the airport to my terminal in Las Vegas and every step of the way I'm texting Nicki explaining my disappointment about the fight and my plans with the guys for next year. I take a break to text my wife I'm boarding so she knows that my flight should be arriving on time. I text Nicki when I arrived at the airport back home to let her know that I got in safe and my wife was picking me up. That was my way to say hey I will talk to you later, she wanted our friendship to remain a secret and I did too, I thought it was best that way for my work and home life, she texted back "glad u made it safe, can't wait to see u!" with a smiley face emoji. I reply Yes ma'am! See you Monday.

I don't know what it is about vacations I always hate when it ends, but that feeling you get when you're back in your own bed is unmatched, there really is no place like your own home. My wife picks me up at the airport with my sons in tote, in the same fashion she dropped me off in. I can see their little heads bobble back and forth watching the sliding doors of the airport hoping the next person is me walking through. They are finally able to make out a figure and recognize me with all my bags, they alert my wife like she's blind and point to me. She smiles and pops the trunk so I can put my bags in the trunk, we kiss and my oldest says "ewww", my youngest joins in right after him. We make our way back home, we talk about my trip, she pretends to be interested in my stories on the car ride home but I could tell she was only making conversation because she didn't want to seem like she didn't care, which she didn't, but I play along. After we get into the house it's early enough for us to figure out dinner plans. As I debate whether I want to go out to eat or order something, I find myself wanting to text pictures of what I got my boys to Nicki, but I didn't want to jeopardize my peace or my secret so I just wait until tomorrow when I see her at work. Monday comes, Nicki and I light up when we see each other, I couldn't wait to tell her in person about everything, we play it off pretty well at work, because all people need to see is us interact a little too closely and the rumors start. We make time after work to talk, we drive somewhere to meet and talk freely. I update her on everything in the parking lot of a downtown food mart far away from our job but close enough so I can get home in time. Nicki and I never have enough time, that's what her and I always say, as we say our goodbyes, she reaches in for a hug which was a first for us, she tightly embraces me, and I respond by hugging her just as tight.

Chapter VI

Divorce!? Don't do me any favors!

Several months pass from then, as I get back in my daily routine, it's become routine for my routine to get interrupted by Las Vegas so the transition back into my everyday life gets easier with every trip. Life's going well by all accounts, my first born will be in Kindergarten next school year and work is a breeze. We're in a pretty good groove as a family, I enjoy coming home now even more, I make my way to the house anticipating my kids rushing me at the door as they normally do. After a long day of work, I have to say it's great as a husband to be able to go home to your family and relax, before you even get the key in good you hear your kids running to greet you before you walk in, like they were waiting all evening just to hear you turn the key, you open the door and they see you, watching their face light up is the best, then talking to your wife about your day, then hearing about hers, it's one of the simple pleasures in life that I try not to take for granted.

Door opens, "Hey baby". Wife: *Hey, do you know a Nickita Wilson?* I think we all know this part.

Wife: You gone keep lying ain't you, man up and tell the truth, you was man enough to do it, man up and tell the truth.

Me: Ok, listen you the last motherfucka to talk about honesty, we're supposed to have three kids and you wanna talk about honesty, you killed our fucking son, get out my face with that bullshit! She's my friend so what, more of a friend than you've been the past three years.

Wife: *Excuse me? First of all fuck you and that bitch, it's my body not yours and you don't even know if it was a boy or a girl wit' yo' dumbass, there was no need to bring another son in this world to model after yo sorry ass anyway, I'm busy enough unteaching them all the dumb shit they see you do, 'Cause you a sorry ass man you aint shit! You just a sorry ass! Always running to Las Vegas every chance you get!*

Me: Sorry? I handle my business, I provided for you and my kids when yo' ass claimed you were all depressed and couldn't work. I did that shit, me! You wanna be out then be the fuck out I don't care anymore, if it wasn't for my sons I would of never married yo' ass anyway, all the shit I put up with you and yo' sorry ass family they ain't nothing but a bunch of fuckin enablers that's why I don't want my kids around them, that's why yo' hoe ass sister home with all them damn kids, and you can kiss my ass about Las Vegas I go once a year, mainly to get away from yo' ass!

Wife: *It aint fun being around yo' boring ass either all you talk about is fucking sports and leave messes for me to clean up around the house, I fucking work too I'm not your maid, you the biggest fuckin child in here! And keep my family out yo' mouth, you got one mo' damn time to mention them, I aint said shit about yo sorry ass family and that ugly ass ring, you and ya' old ass granddaddy picked out!*

Me: Bitch you got the ring you deserved!

Wife: *Bitch!? I got yo bitch you raggedy motherfucka and some man you are, calling the mother of your children a bitch, wait til' I tell my daddy!*

Me: Maaaaaaaaaaaaaan tell ya damn daddy, you a grown ass woman (mockingly I say) "I'm a tell my daddy". Then I say, I been wanting to whoop his ass anyway, please go tell em'.

It was all coming out. My feelings that night were a rollercoaster of emotions, in the midst of our argument, it's getting even more personal, but just as I feel like I'm starting to win the argument she blurts out "and I'm pregnant again, so argue with that, you fucking asshole!" ....Damn that was a bombshell, I paused to gather myself and say the right words, instantly regret filled my heart but as I get ready to make some form of peace, my anger takes over and I respond, "Oh so you aborting this one too baby killer?". She doesn't even respond, I'm pretty sure she starts tearing up while I'm watching her leave, damn how did everything go so wrong? I should have stopped her that night I wasn't being a good man, even if I might have not been her husband for much longer. When I look back at that moment and how I reacted, I wonder if I ever was a good man to her. I was there physically, monetarily, but in retrospect I may have been absent for her emotionally, too worried about my own feelings and not sacrificing enough of myself to rekindle or better our companionship.

There are a lot of things I regret in my life; I absolutely regret calling my wife a bitch I was wrong for that. No excuses can be made for the words I uttered that night but we were arguing, name calling, and sometimes you say things you regret out of anger, that's why I said what I said, but in no way should I be excused for doing it. There would be two things from that night I truly regret, letting her leave in that state and calling her that name, This argument was a long time coming but it shouldn't have happened that way, I guess we had been avoiding our issues in an attempt to keep the peace and our family together, it was easier to get lost in our kids and work. I found my release at work of all places, talk about work-life balance, I had it at the time, so I didn't see the problem. See in the coming months after my last trip to Las Vegas, Nicki had become my best friend she couldn't replace my boys of course but none of them were back home with me so she became my outlet. She was the only woman I have ever met that I could legitimately talk football with and didn't miss a beat, she knew some historical facts that I didn't even know, she loved football, especially our local team, which was perfect because so did I. We spent a lot of time bonding over sports, she listened when I talked about boxing. We talked about going to a game one day with her sons and my oldest, but we knew it was a fantasy, my wife wasn't about to allow me to go to a football game alone with some woman from work with our boys. My wife didn't really care for the game, so many times it would just be my oldest son and me.

Nicki was what my wife wasn't, just a friend. Sometimes I believe we get caught up so emotionally in our relationships we forget one of the most important parts is just simply being a friend sometimes. The chance of my wife and I being friends was long gone. How could she be upset with someone tending to what she neglected. Her jealousy blinded her to the fact that Nicki and I were just friends. It's not like she didn't meet Nicki before, they never formally met but when my wife brought me lunch on one of her off days, she spoke to everyone including Nicki. So, Nicki was a secret, but it wasn't like I was hiding some steamy sexual relationship for almost two years. We were honestly friends. Many of the times I would've annoyed my wife with sports talk, watching sports, or just things I liked, she didn't have to put up with or pretend to like it because I was able to talk to Nicki. The audacity of her after some of the sneaky things she pulled, I get how it looked, but blowing up at me and not letting me tell my side of the story was unfair. I get it, maybe I wasn't as great to her in years past as I remembered, but some of the behavior and the attitude I got from my wife I didn't deserve. She was never happy to do the things I like and when she did come along, she was a killjoy at every event, meanwhile I had to pretend I loved to go to these boring ass dinner parties every time one of her bougie ass friends wanted to celebrate something, and don't let me look like I wasn't having fun, the night wouldn't end until I admitted how rude I was being. She didn't understand me at all which is why I had a PLATONIC relationship with someone who did. And every bit of that was the god's honest truth..............until that evening in the parking lot when I got back from Las Vegas.

We hugged that evening like I said, and it was innocent until she told me she missed me again, it was different when she said it in person, this time it was intimate. She hadn't let me go yet; she slowly softened her grip on me to take a half step back to look me in the eyes. She asks, "We're just friends?" I pause because I don't know what to say next. Only a few seconds pass without me responding and she says, "because I'm in love with you". It had been a long time since I heard a woman say that to me, not since Melissa. I can see her eyes searching for the response she's wanting. I can't say the words but as she gets closer, I lean in and kiss her. It felt like we were kissing to make up for all the time we missed. I'm not one for kissing and soap opera moments but this wasn't the good morning, good night, hey I just walked in the house peck my wife and I routinely did. This was a kiss we couldn't come back from; words were said we couldn't take back either because as we give our lips a break, I now take a half step back to say, "I love you too". Pandora's box was wide open and we had been tempting fate for long enough, I put my hand on the small of her back, pull her in closer, then my other hand makes its way from around her waist, to her hip then slips to her back pocket, I start grabbing a lot more than back pocket. I'm holding her like she's mine and I'm hers, her hands now loosely around my waist as we start kissing again, her hands make their way up my back to press me in tighter. We take another break from kissing, our eyes are just fixated on each other, then she asks, "What are we gonna do?" "Got dammit!!!" I hate that question I think to myself; I really do. That question usually precipitates a major decision when you're in a predicament, it's never like hey, what are you going to do, buy the lobster or the steak? That's never the scenario, not for normal people anyway, that question what are you, or what are we going to do means you're probably venturing into uncharted territory in life, "Mission success probability: low, chances of survival: high", chance you're about to make the wrong decision and your survival will be in question, likely. I didn't know what I was going to do, so how the hell did I know what we were going to do. She had kids, I had kids, I had a wife. I didn't know anything other than in the coming weeks after I told her I loved her, I meant it.

I know what everyone wants to know, what actually happened with Nicki and I after that kiss, I guess I can give you the details I would never give my wife. Our text messages after the kiss changed considerably, I guess it's call "sexting", everything has a new stupid ass name. She texted me first about the kiss, when we kissed it apparently opened the floodgates, literally and figuratively. "I was so wet when we kissed, I can't wait to put both of my lips on you", that was the first text I got at work, not the usual "hey friend" or "what we eating today?". We ate lunch together every now and then so that would have been normal. I was never going to tell her how hard I was when we're kissing until she sent me that message. I hadn't been that hard from kissing since I was in college, it was good to have that feeling back. After the messages the pictures started, I didn't get caught with those pictures though, I got caught with the bullshit ass selfies of all things, make sure when your deleting pictures you don't want people to see, you delete it out of your trash or recently deleted section, speaking from experience. But anyway, those pictures Nicki sent were the type of advertisement to make you walk in the store and when someone asks can I help you; you think hell nah, I know what I want, THAT! The naked pictures, the back shots she sent, the pictures of her titties were everything I was curious about when I would see her in a tight skirt in the office or whenever I could see her nipples get hard through her blouse. It was good to know that women got aroused at work too, so I didn't feel like such a "dog", she told me how many times she thought about us or a situation we were in and how it made her panties so wet she had to go to the bathroom to dry off, which instantly made me hard when I read her texts at my desk. The sexual tension was building, and all this build up was a path we were on that would ultimately seal our bond and the fate of my marriage. We discussed times and places we could meet but nothing ever really worked out, luckily after a few weeks my wife being a daddy's girl finally benefited me, she said she was going to take the kids to see their granddaddy for the weekend, which really meant I'm a daddy's girl and I want to go spend time with the only man that has ever treated me right. Fine by me, I had plans any motherfucking way! I text Nicki while we're at work to let her know when I could come by to see her and she sent a million smiley face, cucumber, and eggplant emojis followed by a few water emojis, I already knew what time it was.

Friday comes, Nicki and I have this smirk on our face all day at work, every time we walk by each other she bumps me just to touch me, she would make sure she bumped me with the softest parts of her body so I knew it was sexual. I get off from work and before I get into my car, I get a text from Nicki that says "see you tonight" accompanied by more emojis. My wife calls me on my way home to let me know she is all packed up with my boys ready to go, she waits for me to get home from work so I can see them off. They have gone to visit her father before and occasionally I'm forced to tag along but when I don't, I always hate to see her take my boys and this time was no different. I walk in the door and my kids greet me like normal but they ask me if I can't go to granddaddy's house this time can I go next time, guilt starts to creep in but they will be with my wife, it's not like I'm abandoning them, that's what I think to ease my guilt. My wife doesn't antagonize the situation, she knows how I feel about her father, so she interrupts and says, "next time boys". She lets me know they're all packed, and everything is in the car. We make our way to the car while I start rough housing with my boys, my wife breaks it up with a smile on her face and tells them it's time to get in the car, "tell daddy you love him so we can go". "Love you dad!" my youngest says, and my oldest with a noticeably more disappointed tone says, "Love you". The boys reluctantly got in the car. I strap my youngest in the car seat as I give him another little playful nudge and he smiles back. I do a little handshake with my oldest as he shows me he's a big boy and straps himself in. My wife and I stand outside the driver side door and chat about texting when she gets in and what time she will be back. I open her car door and she gets in; I tell her I love her, and I kiss my wife goodbye before she backs out of the driveway. I wonder what she was thinking as our eyes made contact one last time before she pulled off. I wonder if that was the moment she became curious about my behavior? I walk back in and call Nicki, usually we text each other but there was no one home, so I was finally free to do as I pleased. We made plans that week for Friday night, that was the only night I would have free because my wife was coming back Saturday night and for some reason TJ was in town, it was perfect timing though, there was a big fight that weekend so we were going to the local bar to check it out. It never occurred to me to ask why he was in town, I just figured he was coming home to visit, plus I was a little preoccupied with other things.

Later that evening my wife lets me know she and the boys made it safely, she called me while I was drying off from the shower. I keep getting ready as we're talking but she cuts it short to my benefit, I'm pretty sure my wife would have questioned the sounds of me spraying cologne and getting ready in the background. It feels like I'm getting ready for a first date. I make sure everything is on point, just enough cologne, deodorant, I make sure my breath is on point. I'm wearing a t-shirt but a nice one with my dark grey jogging pants and my red sneakers to match my shirt. I don't want to over dress, it's not like we're going out. I give myself one last check and a look in the mirror, I'm ready to go. Nicki let me know earlier she had condoms, so I didn't have to worry about that, it was nothing but a beeline straight to her place. I call my wife while I'm in Nicki's driveway to make sure she's in the bed for the night, after she tells me goodnight, we exchange the normal I love you, I text Nicki and let her know I'm outside. I parked in the driveway next to her car and I can't lie I'm a little nervous, it was new, exciting and I wasn't supposed to be there so that added more pressure to the moment. My heart was beating a bit faster than normal. I told myself this is Nicki why am I feeling nervous, I know her, but that didn't work, the closer I got to her door the faster my heart kept beating. I get to the doorstep and I hear the door unlocking before I even get a chance to ring the bell, she opens the door looking sexier than I would have imagined, hair down, a little makeup but not much. She even smelled better than usual,

171

she had on some combination of strawberry creme smelling perfume or maybe lotion. She had on a tank top and some matching shorts from her college alma mater. I call them shorts but they were more like underwear, she had more upper thigh showing than shorts. She says "hey" and rushes in to greet me with a long kiss then quickly turns around and walks to the living room, presumably for me to get a full look at her body like I didn't already have mental notes from the pictures she sent. When she turns around though, I thought there was a lot showing in the front, her school's name was worn but intact and there was just as much ass showing as there was university name on the back. Damn! Sometimes when you leave things to the imagination it's better, because the way those shorts fit her were better than any naked picture I had received from her to that point. I follow her to the living room and sit down on the couch next to her. "You want something to drink?" she asked, "Nah, I'm good." I reply. Shit everything, I needed was right there in front of me I thought to myself. Then she asks "Well, what you want then?" as she leans in placing her leg over mine. I tell her "everything that's in my hand" as I start rubbing her thigh, slowly creeping up trying to get my hand underneath her shorts. We make eye contact and we both leaned in even closer to start kissing. As we start kissing, she starts rubbing on my dick, I'm as hard as I can get. Once she feels me, she stops kissing me for a moment to look me in the eyes and smile, it was a smile like "yeah I got yo' ass now", and she did, I mean once a man gets hard all logic outside of the task at hand goes out the window. She climbs on top and straddles me on the couch as we continue kissing. I use my hands to grip her ass as she gives a slight moan, she can feel me through my jogging pants like I can feel her. I work my hands up to hurt hips to her waist to get to her shirt, I lift up her tank top and start kissing her breast then I began sucking her nipples, that slight moan now turned into a full on sound of release like the sounds someone makes who's immersed in relaxation and pure pleasure. She begins a mixture of whispering and nibbling on my ear, I can't hear all of what she's saying but I did hear her ask "You wanna go to the back or you want it right here?". She feels my body try to lift up, she stands up and grabs my hand as she leads me through the hallway to her room, the walk to her room is interrupted by me wrapping my hands around her waist and kissing the side of her neck which makes her pause and moan like she did on the couch, I do that one more time as we get to her door, I slide my hands inside the front of her shorts to feel how wet she is. I began playing with her to get her even more stimulated if that is even possible for either one of us at this point. I continue rubbing her clitoris as she puts one hand one the wall and uses the other to reach behind me and press the back of my leg closer so she can feel me pressed up against her. I start to remove my hands from her shorts to turn around and start kissing, but before I can, she grabs my wrist and begins sucking on my fingers that were just in her shorts. Ok, "Pause for the cause.". Oh my god she was a freak! At least that's what she was trying to show me. We make our way to the bed where I noticed the room being lit up only by candles, she had planned to come back here all along. While she's taking off her tank top, I kneeled to take her shorts off while kissing my way down from her stomach to the other lips I hadn't kissed yet. She steps out of her shorts and almost lifts me up trying to remove my shirt. I stand up to finish taking my shirt off and she drops my jogging pants then my briefs. She sits back on the bed and starts stroking me, I slowly push her back so she's lying down and I get on top of her and we began kissing. I stop only to start sucking on her nipples again as she lets out another moan, they're frequent now but her moans get louder and longer as I continue kissing my way down again. I stand up and start playing with her before I stick my dick in.

174

As I enter her, the warm, wet feeling of her wasn't new but it had been a while, at least for her. She lets out a moan loud enough to wake up anybody who would've been sleeping in the house once I'm fully inside of her. As the sex gets more intense, she gets louder, the harder I'm fucking her the more I play with her clit the tighter she becomes like she's about to come, but I think I'm going to come quicker. The sounds she made, me watching her breasts go back and forth with each pump, the sound of our skin touching as I sped up was too much and she was about to knock me out in the first round. I had to get it from the back like I had imagined weeks ago when I got her photos, and plus I couldn't go out like some teenager having sex for the first time. I pull out and she lets out a gasp like what happened, but she realizes what I'm doing as I start kissing around her thighs, I'm going down, which makes her grab the back of my head. She lets out a different noise when my tongue touches her, it's a loud ugh! She arches her back as I begin flicking my tongue around and then I start slowly going in circles. She tells me "that's it, don't stop" followed by "Baby I love you. I reach my hand up to play with her nipple, as I begin going in circles faster and faster. She yells "Fuck! I feel it, I'm about to come!" "I'm coming! I'm coming!". She lets a loud shriek followed by several

175

moans, I keep licking until she lets go of the back of my head and pushes me away. She still moaning as I flip her over to get it from the back, exactly like I had been fantasizing about. As I push her head down by the back of her neck, I grab her waist with my other hand to control her, I stick it back in and she continues to moan as I start going faster and harder, she gets louder with each thrust from behind, her body slapping against me gets louder, the soft spots on her body move back and forth like a wave on an old school water bed, she was so soft. This time it doesn't matter that I'm about to come so fast, I put in work. I go faster and clinch her harder the closer I got to coming. Damn, it wasn't the best sex I've ever had……..but it was the best sex I've ever had, it had been a while since I had it like that, it was probably due to the excitement of something new, the almost two years of fantasizing and anticipating. Which is probably why when I pulled out and came, I overshot, in my excitement I didn't realize I got her arm and not just her ass or her back until she told me when she was in the bathroom cleaning up. I could care less, standing there my dick still throbbing it was a euphoric feeling that could only be matched by her actions when she came out of the bathroom to bring me a towel and she saw I was still hard. It was so good that's all I could think about which kept me aroused, she walks up, wet hand towel in hand and she asks with a bit of surprise "You aint done?" she kisses me again as she began to stroke my dick with the wet towel she brought to clean me up, but it was sensual enough to increase my arousal. Nicki looks at me with a smile and says "I got you", she pushes me on the bed, puts her mouth on me and makes my night, she had already made my night but when a woman does that it makes a man feel special.

After we're done, we're lying there with each other kissing and taking moments to look in each other's eyes, we both knew deep down that these moments may be fleeting but I don't think it mattered much to either one of us as we lay there. We continue to talk and as we tease each other about the sounds we made, I start teasing her about her outdated man catching outfit from college she greeted me at the door in, she fires back "I guess it worked though, so much for those condoms you asked about!". Oh shit, she was right, when she saw my face realizing we forgot to use condoms she started laughing, which made me burst out laughing. She got me, I had nothing to say I was so in the moment I slipped up. The night continues but reality sets in after a while, I have to go. Nicki wants me to stay the night, but I can't, my wife is literally two hours away at my in-laws, Nicki understands when I leave her, but she doesn't like it. After our last kiss before I leave, she asks me with a level of vulnerability I haven't seen from her, "Will this ever be real?". I tell her the truth, I really didn't know, between my kids and wanting my family, that was something I couldn't promise her, I could sense her disappointment to my response but what was I supposed to say? The drive home all I think about is her, her body, and the way she felt on me, add that with the fact I had gotten away with it, I was on a high with that brand-new feeling. I got home feeling like I just pulled off the heist of the year, I have some guilt but it's no match for the feelings I had for Nicki and the way she made me feel that night.

Nicki would be the second and the last woman I had ever fallen in love with, it wasn't my wife, in a perfect world it would have been, for the sake of my kids I wish I had been in love with my wife at some point in our marriage, maybe I could have rekindled things before Nicki and I got this far, but my wishes of what could've been is a mute talking point now that my once harmless, now turned family ruining secret was out. What would happen next, I will refer to kindly as a learning experience of a lifetime, I was in no way prepared for what was to come. First off paranoia began to set in, all that no condom shit felt great. The reality is I knew Nicki, but you never really know someone like that. After I had to dodge sex with my wife for a week or so to go get tested because I had to make sure I didn't bring anything home. That shit snapped me back into reality. The panic I felt just thinking of the ways one night could ruin my whole life, would make that the last time I would be with Nicki in that way...without a condom that is.

Chapter VII

You're in the ring by yourself.

Boxing is not a team sport, but you will always hear a fighter refer to his team, meaning his trainer, cut-man, best friend, hype-man etc. You see a fighter's team with him as he makes his grand entrance to the ring, someone from his team is there to aid him into the ring, a fighter's team is even with him in the beginning once he steps in the ring. The announcer makes a dramatic introduction for the fighter, the national anthem of the fighter's respective country is sung, his trainer puts his mouthpiece in for him, takes his shiny robe off, gives him a pep talk in some cases and then the bell rings ....and he's all alone. Once the action starts for a fighter there is no team it's just you and your opponent. All the talk before the fight, all the interviews, all the millions of fans don't matter once a fighter gets hurt and he's in trouble, his "team" is left helpless watching as he tries to survive. That's what it can feel like when trouble finds its way into your life, yeah you have people in your corner but, it's not happening to them it's happening to you.

At first the prospect of being a bachelor or living like a bachelor again was exciting, it was like a weight was lifted off my shoulders, no more awkward dinners, no more having to explain myself, no more judgement from someone who didn't approve of the way I put up towels, hell I could even drink out of the jug again, this shit was going to be great. My wife moved out fully within a week, when you have family help you, things move fast, I guess they wanted to avoid me because most of her stuff and the kids' stuff was out on a weekday while I was at work. At least the transition with us splitting up was peaceful. I would come home and look at my house and it was empty everything wasn't gone but enough for it to be obvious to me when she fully moved out. I almost didn't recognize the place with their stuff gone. There were a few scattered toys from my boys, but you could tell by the looks of it there was no longer a family here. So, I had my regrets, but this is the ugly side of being unfaithful, the fallout.

You lose things in life but there's always something gained whether it's knowledge, freedom, or a new life, I had all three then I had Nicki. She was right there to cushion my blow, my transition into semi bachelorhood wasn't easy but it was amicable, my wife and I argued through text message but that was to be expected, overall it was peaceful. If I was a wiser man, I would've understood that this was the calm before the storm.

Life wouldn't let me off that easy for my transgressions, I was in the eye of the storm and I didn't even know it. *Mourning Bride,* an English playwright in 1697, before I started writing this book, I would've had no clue about that play or who William Congreve was. He's a legend to me now. I appreciate his wisdom; without it I wouldn't be able to accurately described my wife's state of mind and what was to come. "Hell, hath no fury like a woman scorned." Just a truncated misquoted line from a play my ass, I would say he was a man wise beyond his time, but this shit has been going on forever he was merely describing what men go through when we screw up, it was a warning that many of us don't listen to. When my wife left me, I should have chased her, that would have been the typical thing to do or some may say the right thing to do, but I was overcome with the feeling of freedom not yet realizing what it cost me. The rejection she would feel by my lack of effort to win her back or to be frank about it, not wanting her back, mixed with the feeling of me replacing her with a new woman right under her nose would not go over well as time went on.

After Tarah temporarily moved back in with her father and her stepmom it was a weird mixture of emotions for me. She was still pregnant with my child. I never said this earlier, but I did grow to love her as the mother of my kids and as my wife, I was never in love with my wife but over time feelings change and they can grow. I was caught between really disliking my wife and wanting to see her, partly because I wanted to know how the baby was doing and truth be told I missed her, but I held strong with negative thoughts of what she did in the past when we did see each other, part of it was me rationalizing my wrong doings with myself, so I focused on what she had done so I wouldn't feel like I was as wrong as I was. She went behind my back and so I did what I did. The thing is, it wasn't revenge, I was in love with Nicki, but I was the bad guy that tore my family up regardless of what she did, people aren't really up for excuses when what you did causes your family harm, but when you go down the selfish path of only trying to make yourself feel better it hurts everyone involved, including you in the end.

I'm sure my wife had a mixture of emotions but over time I would only witness her fury. We decided during the first month of separation which puts her just over two months pregnant that we wouldn't see a whole lot of each other if it didn't involve the kids, her logic was she was at home with her father, stepmom and sister, they had enough

183

space and she had enough support to pick up the slack with me not being there. She didn't need me financially and she always had someone to watch our kids. I agreed with her plan because at this point, I didn't want an argument and the one time I did go to her parent's house I wasn't welcomed in. They watched me in the driveway through the window like that iconic photo of Malcom X peeking through the curtains with an assault rifle. I don't know if her father was armed, they were ready for a problem, but I wasn't going to give them one, I was just there to pick up my kids. I was removed from the situation, I didn't have to deal with her family anymore, it was just the matter of my kids. As I give in to all my wife's demands just to move on, she begins to become more difficult. See I thought happy wife happy life, give her what she wants, and she won't cause any problems, I guess that rule only applies when you're not with another woman in your spare time. We weren't together but she still felt possessive over me, she knew where Nicki stayed. The very same way she knew I was at her house those nights, it was also the way she knew I was still seeing her, my phone GPS. Phone companies and all these new apps are really trying to get people caught up. Here I was thinking I'm a free man and I get text messages that say, "I know you at that bitches house!" While I was literally at her damn house on the couch. It would get to the point where my kids would become collateral damage, she would say yeah we can meet up here so you can see the kids and she would never show, I went weeks without seeing my kids I had never been more than five or six days without seeing them and even then I talked to them or faced timed them. I couldn't speak to them a lot of times while she was at work because they were with her family when she wasn't home. It got to the point where our text messages were no longer amicable but a session of blame game, laced with profanity and name calling. So much for my peace, but I did still have Nicki to confide in. Nicki tried her best but what can you do when the problem is bigger than you, there was nothing she could do which would ultimately start to cause problems with her and I, especially after she found out my wife showed up to the job. I was in a full-on soap opera, my estranged wife pregnant of four months, showed up to my job trying to confront Nicki, what the hell had my life become. I pleaded and made whatever deal I could make to keep my wife away from my office, here I am in the parking garage at work trying to do everything in my power without pissing her off to diffuse the situation. "I don't wanna fight her, I just wanna let that ugly bitch know what kind of basic ass homewrecking hoe she is!" my wife says loudly, as I try to keep her from going into the office. Man look I will give my wife this, she is a professional woman, but people can be completely different in their personal life, here she is at my job, pregnant ready to put all our business out there like we're on a damn talk show, but tomorrow she'll probably be in a lab coat treating patients with them none the wiser that her ass is crazy. This shit was stressful, I can't even bring up the fact she's playing keep away with my kids while she's in the parking garage to make a point because as long as she was at my job, she held all the cards. I beg and I plead with her before we attract too much attention, and everyone notices us. I'm able to convince her to go home but not before someone from my building sees and it starts getting circulated around the office that my wife and I are having trouble. Nobody truly knew what the argument was about, but Nicki wasn't dumb, she knew what my wife came up there for. Things really came to a head when Nicki returned home from work and she noticed all her Christmas decorations on her door were missing. She texted me to see if I know anything about it like I was possibly playing a joke. "You messed with my Christmas decorations in my yard?" is the text I get. I'm confused, I don't know what the hell she means until she explains all her decorations from her door including her reef are gone and that someone is messing with her. I knew what she was really asking, she wanted to know if my wife had come by and mess with her shit. So, I texted my wife and the response I get is a "LOL", that's all the confirmation I needed to know if she had been there or she had someone go by there and do it. I can't really fuss or start trouble with my pregnant wife about it, to the annoyance of Nicki which creates more problems for us, combined with the fact that I still don't have the time I want with my kids and it's the holidays, things just seem to come crashing down on me all at once.

I never really understood depression, growing up most of my life was just the normal ups and downs, I had no chemical imbalance, I had no family history of it. I heard people talk to me about depression and I gave them advice of what I would do, but for me to get depressed I figured it would take so much that it would be obvious. I believed I would recognize it and I would know when I needed help, or I could just fix it. The holidays can be a stressful time, I never experienced it though, I always had my family of some sort but the holidays were approaching and with Nicki and I having issues over my wife's antics and me not seeing my kids, that freedom I enjoyed so much didn't seem like freedom at all anymore. If Nicki and I took a break from each other, it wasn't like I had ZO, TJ or Marcus right there with me or for that matter my sons. Work was no longer a refuge for me either, once you start dating someone from work that goes out the window, especially when issues arise. I had my grandfather and my pops but I'm my own man at this point, I didn't need their judgment making things worse. Looking back on it I should have taken time out to speak to someone like I advise my friends and family to do when they have rough times. We hear this all the time; men don't go seek help because we think we can handle it or we're too ashamed to admit we need help. I found out getting older for most men is a process of life proving to us we aren't superman, lesson by lesson, which was a fact I was slowly and painfully learning. I was upside down; things were all out of order in my life and when you're not thinking straight you just stay mired in a mess. The house that felt so open and free without someone nagging me, now felt like confinement, man I really messed up I thought to myself. It was one day after work when Nicki and I weren't going to see each other. I went home to an empty house; my wife had the kids and I was alone just sitting and thinking. Remember earlier when I talked about the heartbreak a fighter causes his fans when he loses, I left out a very important part and that's how the fighter feels. You can see it on their face after a loss, some fighters don't stay for the post fight interviews to hide it, I've even seen fighters breakdown and cry. The dejection and shame a fighter must feel after he or she suffers their first loss looks devastating, many fighters go through depression, they can't believe they lost, being the best is who they were and now that's in question, they question themselves. They have the public shame of losing a fight, a major blow to their ego. Some fighters carry their whole family and the hopes and dreams of an entire nation in the ring with them, the thought of letting down their biggest fans must haunt them, it's just a cacophony of emotions. Which is what I was feeling, it was going to be public knowledge soon that my marriage had failed, the questions, the how, and the why, I didn't want to suffer through and on top of that I too had let down my biggest fans, my kids. My sons not understanding, and the questions they asked hurt me a lot, but it was my fault so to some degree I had to be honest with them on a level that they would understand. I wasn't honest with everyone though, in the midst of all this turmoil in my life were the phone calls and the group texts with Marcus, TJ, and

ZO. I never mentioned a word to my closest friends, it was my business, my secret, and what could they do anyway, yes, sometimes it is good to have a listening ear but I didn't want to talk about that in the moments we were cracking jokes, talking boxing, or discussing our next trip to Las Vegas, it was a secret I needed to hold on to because I figured I could handle it and I was a little embarrassed, but I wouldn't be the only one in the group holding on to a secret.

Early in December I get a call from TJ, we're talking the usual, boxing, work, then out of nowhere he tells me his mom died a few days ago. Although it registered, I couldn't say anything but damn. I wondered what the circumstances were but that's not a thing you ask, you let a person in grief give you the information they want you to have. He spoke in his usual tone but something like the death of your mother has to cut a person deep, that's the thing about grief and depression, some of your friends can be great actors, hiding their ailments so well, I found out later that his mother was admitted to the hospital after our most recent trip to Las Vegas, his mother had a run of the mill doctors visit, but her doctor ended up admitting her that day because of unforeseen complications, he goes on to tell me that she would spend the next six months in the hospital getting better, then getting worse, he had been on a roller coaster much like I was but he hadn't done anything wrong, life just happened as it sometimes does. The rest of TJ's year would consist of him coming back home every couple of weeks to check on her while she was in the hospital in between figuring out how to balance school, work, and money issues, while not saying a single word to me, ZO, or Marcus. He planned Las Vegas with us like normal, he joked like normal, none of us saw this coming. I was holding a secret that was eating me up but with TJ's news I realized we all need someone to talk to. Most men deep down feel like we got it, but I know I didn't and neither did TJ. When we came to support him at the funeral it was surreal, one because I knew his mother and two, I saw something I never thought I would see in my life, it was TJ, and he was crying. So many times, we've been sitting around having a good laugh and of course TJ was having the best laugh of us all, he loved to laugh. He would laugh so hard he would cry, and someone witnessing it for the first time would ask one of us, "Is he crying?" , he would respond in between laughing hysterically and drying his tears with his hands "Yeah man that shit was too funny" then start laughing again. That was TJ and at any given time you could find tears in his eyes from laughter. But these tears were different, I had never seen these tears from TJ. As we stood outside on by all other accounts a beautiful December afternoon. The tears coming from TJ were the type of tears that never dry, you couldn't just wipe them away with your hand, dry them with a handkerchief, no these tears were the type of tears you had to eventually cover up with a smile because nobody is supposed to cry forever, although the hurt is permanent. The tears on TJ's face were the type of tears that if you ever looked closely behind someone's smile, you would see them permanently nestled in the crevices and wrinkles we wear as we age.

I'm reminded of a quote I once read in passing, forgive me I don't know who to give credit to, it's not verbatim but it went something like this, *"Sympathy only last for a while, while grief can last forever."* My situation was different, I cried my tears to be honest, and my disappointment would last forever but not my tears. The tears I cried in my private moments were not because of loss, I did lose my family, but my tears came from the realization of the absolute failure of a marriage that sat in my lap and the strain it placed on my children. Remember what I said earlier about my coworker John and the young lady he was sleeping with at work, that I had only heard of shitty husbands that cheated on their pregnant wife. It was in those moments of self-reflection I realized I shouldn't judge because however the circumstances or explanation, I was now that guy. I was having an active affair while my wife was carrying what is now my beautiful baby girl. Life has taught me many things, not to be too self-righteous or judgmental being tops on that list, but I think pride is the last thing to go and that's probably true for all men, even with the news of what TJ had been going through and my acknowledgement that I was depressed, I never talked to anyone not even my best friends. Even after TJ opened up somewhat one early afternoon a few months after the funeral. TJ never really talked about how he felt or how he was doing. TJ calls me and he begins to speak about his mother, TJ: *Man bruh it's crazy I have been telling my sister to get out that headspace of being down and thinking about our mom too much, but man sometimes that shit backfires when you try to block it out. I got off work early today, took care of some other shit and man, it's a beautiful day today, so without really thinking bruh, because I was in such a good mood I say let me call this old lady and see what she's up to, I was in such a good mood that day and it had been so long since I felt like that, man I fucking forgot she was gone, it hit me immediately ain't no more phone calls man, ain't no more*

193

jokes, I can't help with the bills anymore, she's gone. There was a short pause. TJ had been sending money home and helping out his mom since he was able to in undergrad, he kept helping until she passed, he had always hoped he would make it big in something, so he could finally have her living carefree and well taken care of but worrying about money and making something out of himself turned in to missed time with her and he was out of time and none of that mattered anymore. I could tell when he paused TJ might have started to get emotional, but he quickly changed his tone and said "Man, it will be our day one day, I'm just thankful to see another day B." I agreed and then TJ turned the conversation to Las Vegas and when my baby girl was due.

My baby girl got here in March, I remember thinking about how immature I was when I was so proud of myself that I made two boys, standing there holding my baby girl I was just happy that she was here and she was healthy, I was in love. I was going to be her protector, her best friend her everything, much like I was for my boys, but this was different, this was my little girl. Being at the hospital wasn't as awkward as I anticipated, I guess the joy of a new life in the family calmed everyone's nerves, my in-laws softened their attitudes towards me, her father and I shook hands but not much was said, it wasn't necessary either, it was one of the few moments of understanding between him and I. I think in that moment he understood my frustration with him and his interference in our marriage or at least I hope he did. The handshake wasn't an apology more so of a truce, I spent the rest of the time with my wife and the baby, in between that her stepmother and I had friendly conversations, she was always the most understanding of them all, of course her sister treated me like I was the worst person in the world but that was to be expected, she was the most difficult one to deal with of all my wife's family throughout this whole process, texting my phone, sending me messages on social media. I'm pretty sure my wife told her everything I said about her. My wife and I interacted better. I was her husband again for a moment, alerting the nurses when she needed something or going to get it myself, I owed her that much at least. I even made her laugh when I came in the door with the extra blanket, juice, and water she requested, I bumped into the door and almost dropped everything but I clung on for dear life keeping everything in my hand so I didn't have to go back. She chuckled at my balancing act, she could tell I was trying, we did have our moments together. I thought things had calmed a little, we begin talking about how she was feeling, and how beautiful our baby girl was, it was like we forgot we were getting divorced right up until she said, "and you better not have that bitch around my baby". It became apparent to me in that moment that no matter what, Nicki and I may never know peace because my wife would always hold a grudge. During the first couple of months of my daughter's life I spent more time at my in-laws, I was actually welcomed in the house, this meant I was spending more time with my wife. Tarah and I briefly entertained the idea of getting our family back together but it just wasn't in me, I wasn't in love with her, we weren't friends or lovers anymore we were co-parents, she knew it too but I guess we figured it was worth a conversation. When she wasn't concerned with Nicki, we got along with each other better than we ever did when we were together. As my wife and I were coming to an agreement on a schedule so I can see my children regularly, Nicki became less and less patient with me, she put pressure on me about being over my in laws house so much, she said she understood, she would even tell me "It's great you're getting time with your kids now." but I could tell it bothered her. Nicki would take her frustrations out on me in different ways, she had an attitude every time we spent a little time apart because she knew where I was, so sex was out of the question which caused more tension. Then there was the elephant in the room, Nicki wanted to be in a committed relationship. To be honest this is what happens when you don't think things through, the wiser me understands that now. I had never given much thought to what a relationship would look like between us, it became real once we started having problems. I was technically still married and that ate at her, she started to get more territorial, she wanted to know where I was more, and it made me realize I was potentially hopping out of the frying pan into the fire. The reality is anyone that has ever gotten out of a relationship and then met someone new will attest to the fact that there's always issues and there's always baggage eventually. It wasn't a case of the grass being greener. I knew I never wanted to be with my wife again but was I ready to be the man Nicki wanted me to be. This would be the first time I thought in those terms, because I knew now that when you take on a task you aren't ready for it can go terribly wrong for everyone involved. The reality was, I had been a husband and a father before I was ready, and I needed time, not to know what type of man I wanted to be, eventually I wanted a wife and to be settled down but to know when I was ready to be that man, I needed that time and I needed that time to myself. The selfish me thought maybe I could have the woman I was in love with and figure out when I was ready, but I knew deep down that wasn't going to work. I spoke earlier to you about what it's like when someone is paying you close attention, especially someone you're romantically involved with; they get accustomed to your habits so when the smallest thing is different, they notice. The changes that naturally occur when you become distant with a significant other, is nothing we do intentionally but it will set off alarms like it's deliberate, especially when your hiding something. When you cut conversations shorter, you don't react the same way to the things you loved about them, you don't kiss the same, or just seem to be in deep thought more often instead of having a conversation with them, it screams trouble. I was fresh off a life lesson experiencing that very fact. Me being wiser after my monumental mess up, I knew how much trouble and headache lay ahead for Nicki and me, especially with my kids being held as a bargaining chip by my wife, she didn't want our kids around Nicki at all. At any point and time my wife could decide to keep my kids from me if she suspected I was around Nicki or if she simply got in a sour mood about our history, for the first time in my life though, I was really ready to sacrifice for love. See I understood the error of my ways, love involves sacrifice. Sacrificing when it's necessary is not an emotion, it's not just feeling like you love someone but showing it. Being honest with myself I couldn't recall the last time I truly sacrificed for anyone. My kids loved me by default because I was dad. I let my wife down because I made poor choices, it was time to finally man up and sacrifice for love. So, I did, it was a hard conversation to have but I told Nicki that her and I could no longer be, it would hurt my kids and I was done doing that. I let go of the woman in my life that I was in love with, and this would be the second time. But this time was different, I let go of a companion and a lover that meant so much to me to have what meant most to me, my kids. The discussion between Nicki and I was not void of emotion, we both had our moments, but she respected my decision. I think at some point we both saw it coming, but what can you do with fools in love, they're hardheaded and that's exactly what we were. Nicki and I never said our goodbyes because we would see each other at work, which was going to be difficult, but the basis of our whole relationship was the fact that we were truly friends. The coming weeks and days at work were awkward but natural in appearance, we were still a secret to the office, but when I got the news that I was transferring across town, she was the most emotional of all my coworkers at my going away celebration, if they didn't suspect anything before, they would now have ammo to gossip. Honestly, I don't know what would've happened if I had stayed, but luckily life sometimes, and by life, I mean God or whatever other outside forces anyone believes in, saves us from ourselves. Nicki and I vowed to remain friends and keep in contact, but me being years wiser and much more of a realist than that young inexperienced college kid, I understood however well-intentioned we were with the words we spoke; we would inevitably be out of each other's lives completely. The breakup didn't wear as hard on me as my impending divorce did prior to my daughter being born. I've had to let go of the woman I loved in Melissa before, so I wasn't new to losing love. I had spent the holidays as a guest with my kids. I had become familiar with the feeling of disappointment and heartbreak. I wasn't numb to what happened with Nicki and I, but I wasn't the same man I was in years past, which made my transition to being a bachelor easier than it would have been without my previous failures. Combine my failures with the presence of my new baby girl along with the opportunity to see more of my kids, and Las Vegas being around the corner, I was going to be just fine. There was just one problem, TJ.

We had all been in communication about Las Vegas for close to a year, we literally start planning the next trip before we leave Las Vegas, it's just always based on the upcoming fight around Cinco de Mayo, hotel flights were being worked out but I was never staying with TJ again after the porno girl incident so I didn't think of him not having plans to stay with anyone until I didn't hear from him as the date got closer. I call him just to make sure he has everything in order, TJ is usually the first to have his flight booked, and his hotel locked in. He was late to everywhere we went except for Las Vegas, so it was odd he hadn't said anything. That thing about grief lasting a lot longer than sympathy, well that was TJ, we volunteered to pay for his flight, I wouldn't even mind us rooming together again if it meant he was coming, but he didn't have it in him this time, we were going to be a man down this year. The reality of not having TJ there didn't really hit until we all met up. It didn't feel right, I could only imagine what he was going through privately to not make it here with us, Marcus called to let him know that he was missed, he had to talk tough so after that Marcus told him "Let this be the last time you miss a trip with yo bitch ass!", then he heard us yelling in the background "Yeah wit yo bitch ass!". ZO forever the shit talker said, "Don't worry y'all he coming this Mufucka just late as usual.". We all bust out laughing including TJ, for a moment we were all there. I think that laugh did TJ some good, but it would never change the fact that his mother was gone, nor would it change the fact that he wasn't with us in "the Caf". Las Vegas was our home away from home, time always stood still when we came back. Every time we came back if felt we were just there last month, same lights, same strip but it was different this time and it wasn't for the best.

Chapter VIII

Fool me once.

"Fool me once, shame on......shame on you. Fool me......you can't get fooled again." All things considered; George Bush is probably remembered more favorably than most people would have ever predicted. I personally love that quote from "W", some people see it as a hatchet job on an old saying, I see it much different, I think that's exactly what people say after they feel like they got railroaded in a relationship. You say to yourself "I can't let that shit happen again no matter what" and that's exactly what old "W" meant, but That wasn't my initial thought as I returned back home from Las Vegas to an empty apartment, no my first thought was the stinging realization of how empty everything felt. My cousin picked me up from the airport and dropped me off home to an empty bachelor pad. For a second talking to him on the ride to my apartment made me forget I was coming home to unwanted solitude. Walking through the door was a hard dose of reality, there were no kids waiting on me, no wife to greet me with open arms and a peck on the lips, that now seemed way more intimate than ever before because now there was no one for me to kiss back. I had to wait to give my kids their new boxing souvenirs. That evening I got back from Las Vegas it felt like the holidays all over again when I realized I didn't have my family. I didn't slip into full on depression, but it was an emotional moment, I couldn't blame anyone about how I was feeling but myself. This apartment wasn't home. I always felt like there was nothing better than coming home to my own bed off of a week-long vacation, but maybe it wasn't the bed, maybe it was the wife I took for granted, maybe it was OUR bed, maybe it was the kids I always expected to be there that made it home, yeah that had to be it. The way I felt that night when I returned to my apartment, we could've all been crammed into the one bedroom I just moved in and it would have felt like home, anything would have felt like home as long as they were there, but that was never to be again. A couple of months later our divorced was finalized and she had her place and I had mine, on the bright side I did have my kids on a regular basis now, but watching my sons adjust to our new normal didn't make me feel like the world's best dad like the mug and T-shirt read, that my boys picked out for me one Father's Day. I bet now you might be wondering where does the you getting railroaded part come in, you cheated, you tore your family up that's what you get, yes that all may be true, I messed up bad. It would have been better to end our marriage under more honorable conditions, but it's a strange headspace to be in when you've always wanted your family more than you ever wanted your spouse. We may have been doomed from jump but neither one of us were wise enough to see it. See when I speak of being railroaded, I'm referring to the mistakes I subjected myself to as a younger man because I was ill prepared for the task I was undertaking. I won't let that shit ever happen again. When I think about everything I put myself through, I learned some valuable lessons, and that is you can't rush maturity, it takes time to evolve, it takes time to learn how to be an adult let alone know how to successfully be with another person, when I was younger I can honestly say I was not ready for marriage I was still too immature, still too selfish. When it's put this way, it makes you think. When you're in your twenties especially your early twenties you have spent way more time as a kid than being an adult and much of your transition at that time is spent unlearning the ways of a child so it's a difficult task to learn how to be an adult with someone else who may perceive and process information differently than you do. You would think someone would've given me that advice, but even if someone did, I already knew everything, when you're young you think you know it all; you think it's different. Like my nephew, I now understand how I made the mistakes I made by watching my nephew grow into an adult and make his own mistakes. I found myself being the voice of reason to my own nephew. He calls himself fresh out of high school going to the military because he thought it was a bright idea for him and his high school sweetheart to get married. I told him " Sean she's young, you're young, it's possible it can work out but not likely, neither one of you is close to growing into the adults you're going to be and when she becomes a woman, that fully matured woman, what if that woman doesn't want you. See there's a common misconception that women mature so much faster than men, and that is nowhere near the truth, women can develop certain qualities and traits faster than men because of societal influences and vice versa but emotional maturity and wisdom are not bestowed on one sex faster than the other when it comes to romantic relationships. Emotions for both sexes run high and rash decisions are often the result, which is why I pleaded with my nephew to rethink his course of action, but what did he do, what every young person does, not listen. He swore into the military, proposed to her and presented her with an engagement ring. Wouldn't you know it, a few weeks before he was supposed to ship off she told him maybe it wasn't a good idea to join the military and things may have been moving too fast, she was right but she was also the one who brought up the whole marriage idea. She brought up marriage to ease her frustration with the distance she didn't believe she could handle. She watched him join the military, buy a ring, she even said yes, and then she had a moment of clarity. That happens so many times when we're young, clarity comes after promises and decisions are made. My nephew was embarrassed, my sister and I, his father everyone warned him, but he was determined to prove us wrong, See what he didn't understand we had all been there before and we wanted better for him, he wanted better as well but he just didn't know better. Nobody was pregnant, there was no one breathing down his neck for a ring or pressuring him to make a decision, he had a chance to be a young man with all of life's options at his disposal. He was too young to understand this concept, and that is, if she's the woman that's meant for you, and you're meant for her and marriage is forever then what's the damn rush? I wish I understood that concept, a lot of the ways I would think about things now or the way I would approach situations or even talk to women are a far cry from how I would have done things at twenty one, twenty two, twenty three years old. At that age I didn't understand things like postpartum depression, I didn't understand there were a lot of ways I could have built my wife up instead of tearing her down and causing more rancor and strife within our household, but that's life when you're young. You don't truly understand the task at hand, so you put too much on your plate when you honestly don't know a damn thing about being a partner. Me not knowing anything about relating to women, understanding women, how to be a husband, balancing that with being a father and nurturing a baby were things I had to learn with time after I was able to reflect on the path I took that steered my marriage into a ditch.

I've always heard poor communication can ruin a relationship but it's hard to recognize it when emotions are running high and you're more concerned with the wrong that was done to you. Good communication, simple concept, hard to execute. The powers of poor communication are limitless, that wall of poor communication can become a barrier when it comes to finances, family, not being able to pursue your dreams which ultimately caused my relationship to deteriorate even more. I learned a lot from my experience, like it takes time for most people to learn how to express themselves, when you are in your early twenties you genuinely don't know how to express yourself, the right way to express yourself or the most productive way to express yourself. Over time you start to learn those tools to cultivate better and healthier relationships but not before you've made a few mistakes. I don't have any regrets about getting married at such a young age or having kids at such a young age, but I can honestly say I wasn't ready, I didn't have the tools to effectively communicate in a way that would have produced a long standing and healthy marriage. It's not just lip service when people say communication is key. Also, I think you must be willing to sacrifice, go to counseling if he or she asks, go on vacations, relationship conferences. You might want to take all measures to keep a good line of communication open because in my case our communication broke down so early that I just thought that's how things were going to be with no chance of getting better. Ultimately, I started communicating with someone outside of my marriage and me being young and dumb, I didn't understand the fatal mistake I was making in my marriage by giving my communication to another woman, but I've learned now, it was just the hard way. I wasn't as fortunate to learn a valuable lesson without consequences like Marcus did in Las Vegas and neither was ZO. One thing I've known for a fact even when I was younger is that it's wise to take the opportunity to learn from other people's mistakes. ZO like many people misunderstood what a relationship is all about. Nobody is owed a companion, I'm willing to bet you can travel to almost anywhere in the world and you won't find the exact same number of eligible women and men to pair off, so what does that mean. It means it's a game of musical chairs and someone is going to get left out, so be thankful someone has chosen to spend their time with you. Time is the most valuable thing we have and there's no way to make more of it or stop it, so the time someone is giving you is them giving you their best, it may not always be their best moments but it's what they have. I know possessiveness and a moderate amount of jealousy can make someone feel wanted and some may say it's even healthy, but I think a lot of us like ZO go too far. As men, we tend to judge a woman too harshly on where she's been, how many people, and how that makes us feel, but in the end what does it really matter? Same can be said for women in this way, ladies when you love him or you really like him stop being so damn hard on him because he doesn't fit in that box of the ideal man you think you deserve and his habits work your nerves, ask yourself is it really that bad? Yes, he's a little messy, but damn the dirty clothes are at least around the clothes hamper this time even if they didn't make it all the way in, I bet you can remember when he used to leave his nasty ass draws anywhere in the room, now he's trying to hit a bank shot off the wall to make it in the hamper, that's progress! I'm willing to bet my last dollar, ladies some of you are just as annoying. My question is, what does that matter when you have someone of worth in front of you, to help you get through the hurt of losing a loved one? What does it matter when he or she is there to tell you, you are valuable, after the world or your "9 to 5" makes you feel like you ain't shit? What does it matter in your most vulnerable moments, when you have someone to help you stay strong and let you know baby you can do it, I believe in you? I think in the grand scheme of things those small grievances don't matter to most people when it's thought about that way, because you realize having a companion is a gift, not a right. I think that's the concept that most people miss, it's a privilege to get someone's time and the person receiving it should feel so. We only have our companions for so long. I would think it'd be wiser to criticize less and enjoy more of the limited time you have with the one you love before the option is taken away and all your left with is what if's and what could've been, because believe me when I say

211

this, even if you choose not to believe me on anything else I've said, one way or the other the time will come and the reality will be either you or your loved one will be out of time, whether it's through death, divorce, or sickness there's just never as much time as you think. The truth is we don't own anyone's body, their mind, or their heart, they can only share it with us. I believe it's best practice to remember when you want to harp on a person's past, focusing on the mistakes they've made and you're struggling to forgive them, that it's important to realize that a healthy relationship is companionship not ownership, they're sharing themselves with you and you have privilege with them not control, they'll never be the exact way you want them to be, so instead of always expecting them to be different you should try to be better at being understanding.

Now would you look at me, sounding all philosophical and shit, you would think I got it all figured out right? I don't, I'm still learning. After some time, I got adjusted to being a bachelor and I'm dating again. Nicki naturally found someone else and those text message replies slowed until finally they stopped after she let me know she had a new man, which I completely respect, life goes on, but let me say this, man I thought marriage was tough. Dating in your thirties is giving marriage a run for its money, sweet baby Jesus, Mary, and Joseph! It's a wild ride, like a scary ass roller coaster and you got the one seat where the seatbelt doesn't click all the way. Which makes me truly thankful for my past because now I'm better equipped to handle a relationship, I'm able to be honest with myself about when I want to be committed and when I don't, but being honest with the woman I'm involved with about it, that on the other hand, that's not always as easy as I thought it would be, but I'm maturing........in a lot of ways.

Lust is still pretty good at disguising itself as love, I mean lust is walking around in a damn business suit in the bank greeting people and after you ask your question and give her your account number, she lets you know "Oh bitch I don't work here I was just looking for somebody!" To my credit I have avoided a lot of my old mistakes but there's always new ones to make. The reality of dating in your thirties is the fact that a lot of women I meet are going to have kids and I can't judge them, shit I got kids too and a story to go with it. Kids add a completely different wrinkle in your dating life, it's tough for any parent that's trying to do the best for their kids, to balance dating, and parenthood.

The funny thing about raising kids is you have to set rules you break. For instance, I know growing up there wasn't locking any bedroom doors in my house, my father and stepmother weren't having it. I'm raising my kids the same way "Uh Uh, unlock that door and keep it open so I can see what y'all doing in there!" I can't believe I say that now. As a parent, sometimes you must keep your doors locked so they don't know what you're doing. My ex-wife and I knew that, we had a game plan, whether it was wrapping Christmas presents or sex, but everyone has their own way of doing things, which was apparent once I started dating again. I met a woman online, yes online don't judge me, I don't have the time like I used to, to be out scouting in the club, it wasn't one of those free sites though, this site you had to be on there looking for something substantive. But anyway, we go on a few dates, we start texting like new romantic interest do, so when I got a late-night text at 1am to come over and my kids were with my wife that night, I got dressed and I was on two wheels over there. She answers the door in a robe and I already know what time it is, we head to the room and we start kissing then we eventually make it to the bed, as I began to get into it we start making more noise and she tells me "shhh you have to be quiet, my boys are asleep."

Which doesn't throw me off because I had been married, so I knew the struggle of trying to quietly have sex and not wake the kids. What did throw me off however, is when the door creaked open and a little boy, says "Oh my god!", I thought maybe her kids were at their dad's house initially. Poor little man, I guess he couldn't sleep, she had two boys and the youngest one, the six-year-old wanted to sleep in the bed with her. Her youngest son expected simply just to walk in and climb into bed like usual, instead to his horror, he walked in to see nothing but my bare ass. Her oldest son still sleep or playing sleep never came out of his room. All she could do is yell out instructions to him and scramble so she could hide under the covers, "Close ya eyes! Close ya eyes! and close the door!". So he closes his eyes and closes the door, but poor kid he was still in the room, he was so flustered, meanwhile I've already moved to cover myself up and she yells "Get out the room and close the door!" her son responds "Momma I can't see!" he still had his eyes closed, I would've too. Wrapped up in a blanket she hops up and quickly switches it out for a robe, she says, "Hold on baby, momma sorry.", she ushers him back to bed as he asked, "Can I open my eyes now?" I couldn't help but laugh to myself. She took a while to come back, I know she was doing her best to explain what he just saw, but really what can a parent say at a time like that, there's no parent playbook for that. She comes back and to my surprise she's ready to try and have sex again. Hell, I just knew she was going to tell me to go home, I was counting on it, and if she couldn't read my mind, she could tell by my body's response, limp dicks don't work will with condoms. Welcome to dating in your thirties, we would eventually consummate our courtship, but things didn't end up working out between her and I, but that's another story for another day.

I'm still hopeful I will find that wife and be that husband I saw myself as. So, I welcome a new beginning or a new chapter in my life. I have time to work on myself to be a better man, mentally and physically, I'm even in the gym more, the gym is a great place to meet someone, you never know where your next great love will be, which is exactly what crossed my mind one day when I walked into my gym and saw this sexy girl walking on the treadmill I hadn't seen before. She had a familiar twist in her hips when she walked, she was working out but still trying to be cute. Her back was to me so I couldn't see her face, but physically everything else she had was everything I wanted. I walk around to get a towel, really it's just to get a better look I never use a towel, but today I was using a damn towel, so as I walk over, I try not to be obvious but I'm definitely trying to make eye contact. As I get close enough to get a better look, I couldn't believe it, it was Melissa. She takes out her headphones, "Jae?" we were both in shock, my college sweetheart was in my hometown, it had been years since we last saw each other. We broke up because of the distance and now here she was, it was easing my mind that she had a smile on her face as she stepped down off the treadmill to greet me. We could've talked forever. Can this be real? I'm hopeful it is, after all my early trials and failures I think love just may have a place for me, and if love has a place for me after all the mistakes I've made, it definitely has a place for you. So, when love knocks you down, and it will. When love hurts so bad you don't know if you can continue, because it will. When people are watching as you're being counted out after love has decided to hand you yet another heart stopping blow, because it will. Take a deep breath, gather yourself, rise to your feet, bite down on your mouthpiece and keep swinging for the fences, because sometimes in love just like in the fight game, that's how winning is done. God bless and thank you so much for reading.

Final Thoughts

The end. That's what I thought I was going to feel like as I put the finishing touches on this story. The funny thing is, this isn't it, I wanted to just write a book as a one off, just to tell a funny story, a collection of funny events I've experienced. As I began writing I realized the natural arc and crest of the story lent itself to a whole different book, the whole reason I wanted to write the book is much of what happened after chapter five and I barely got to it. Volume two is a thing, if not to finish the story then simply because I've truly enjoyed this process.

It's an odd but cathartic venture writing a story involving your life, because for it to be a truly captivating story you must reveal a bit of honesty that for many people is only resigned to the thoughts and secrets you hold in your mind. I had to be honest about myself and the way I operated, taking fault when I now have a clear head instead of attempting to prove a point. I wrote this knowing fully that if this book turned out to be something the world may hate Jae Jameis. I may be the subject of heated debates; where was I wrong, what type of man I am? There is the long shot of me being a sympathetic character, but I'm not asking to be, shit what's done is done. But I can't lie, if this book takes off to the point where it sparks debate as a hot topic, Thank you! I mean that shit. Make me as controversial as you want if you purchased a copy and enjoyed yourself, best case scenario, I figured it catches the eye of a few and they take it as a nice little story with a boxing twist.

I was nervous about adding the boxing element into this, I felt like it may potentially alienate some readers, but it was a story I wanted to tell, and I had a unique way of telling it. The analogies weren't just some cool way to think of love or life for me, no I love boxing not because of the violence but more because it can reveal so much of who we are. One of the times I've felt my most helpless is when I first started boxing and I had no endurance for the sport. I looked good for about two rounds, then as I started to tire, the guy I was sparring took advantage, I backed up, I ran, I tried to hold on, but I was a sitting duck, I had never been hit so hard in my life, but I didn't fall. I survived the round. There was nowhere to go while the seconds of the round were still ticking, and my sparring partner was breathing as if he hadn't even started fighting yet. I felt trapped, the walls were closing in and the guy I was fighting wanted payback from when I buzzed him in the first round. For those who aren't familiar with the term buzz in boxing, it means exactly what it means when someone has had a few drinks. I remember in that third round when I was in *dire straits*, absolutely the most tired I had ever been in my life, I was thinking don't quit, don't let this be where you fall, stay on your feet and survive, I'm ok.

Sometimes that's what life is, realizing it sucks, I'm tired but I can go a little longer, I am strong. You look closely enough at a boxing match and it's not just talent or violence, there's emotions, thoughts, game planning and execution involved. I liken it to the best high-speed chest match ever. In so little time you can see a boxer processing his environment, his opponent, you can see if he's timid or he's out of shape or he just isn't good enough, you see what happens when he loses confidence in the tools that have got him thus far. Just for a moment you get a peek into the psyche of the world's toughest competitors and realize they're human like us, every bit as vulnerable and nervous. In a dishonest world the ring reveals all truths, now it may be a different story when deciding the victor, but for the most part people know what they see when they watch a fight. I hear a lot of people say, I watch boxing for the knockouts, knockouts are cool but it's the human story, the drama playing out right before our very eyes with so much on the line, that's what I'm in love with. You can literally watch a man or woman in one single event uplift a country, it's amazing. But boxing is not without its share of tragedies; people are risking it all when they step into the ring. Not to sound dismissive of life or stretch this analogy beyond its limits, but that's love. When love is great, it's amazing but when it goes bad it can feel tragic or even be tragic in some awful cases. So, for me this analogy was a life time of thought and experience nothing random, see I made mistakes, I learned some lessons, and I got put on my ass, but with all that I'm still standing and well enough to leave the story on a good note, I ran into Melissa, the first love of my life, my college sweetheart, and once my college sweetheart always my college sweetheart......right?

In Loving Memory of
Cathy L. Johnson
February 13th, 1953 to December 4th, 2016

Acknowledgements

Special thank you to my friends and family for giving me honest feedback and the motivation to keep going. Very special thank you to the MGM Hotel and Casino and the great city of Las Vegas. Also thank you to ESPN for their willingness to invite fans to their live broadcasting events, allowing us the opportunity to meet the network's talent specifically; Max Kellerman, Stephen A. Smith, Cari Champion, and Michelle Beadle. Thank you to Freddie Roach for always being a great ambassador to the sport of boxing by treating fans with respect. Credit to Mike Tyson for his famous quote "Everybody has a plan until they get punched in the mouth.", the inspiration for my cover art. Thank you to all the boxers and boxing personalities who signed autographs and took pictures with a regular guy that admires what you all do. That includes but not limited to: Tommy Hearns, Johnny Tapia (RIP), Winky Wright, Keith Thurman, Canelo Alvarez, Manny Pacquiao, Roy Jones Jr., Anotnio Tarver, Errol Spence jr., Terrence Crawford, Zab Judah, Lennox Lewis, Evander Holyfield, Kelly Pavlik, Naazim Richardson, Floyd Maywether Sr., Sergio Mora, Paulie Malignaggi,Sugar Ray Leonard, Sugar Shane Mosely, James Toney, Bob Arum, Andre Ward, Teddy Atlas, Brandon Rios, Bermane Stiverne, Roberto Duran, Ruslan Provodnikov, Floyd Mayweather Jr. and countless others. Thank you to friend and editor Alycia Cox, and you, the reader! Last, but not least, thank you Harold Lederman may you rest in peace thank you for taking time out to joke with me and take a picture with a fan. The humility you showed as I thanked you for taking time out to speak with me and your smile will never be forgotten, you were part of the soundtrack to some of the most exciting events I've experienced.

Made in the USA
Lexington, KY
07 December 2019